SHADOW RIDER:
APACHE SUNDOWN

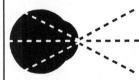

This Large Print Book carries the
Seal of Approval of N.A.V.H.

SHADOW RIDER: APACHE SUNDOWN

JORY SHERMAN

THORNDIKE PRESS

A part of Gale, a Cengage Company

GALE
A Cengage Company

Farmington Hills, Mich • San Francisco • New York • Waterville, Maine
Meriden, Conn • Mason, Ohio • Chicago

Copyright © 2007 by Jory Sherman.
Shadow Rider #2.
Thorndike Press, a part of Gale, a Cengage Company.

Thorndike Press® Large Print Western.
The text of this Large Print edition is unabridged.
Other aspects of the book may vary from the original edition.
Set in 16 pt. Plantin.

LIBRARY OF CONGRESS CIP DATA ON FILE.
CATALOGUING IN PUBLICATION FOR THIS BOOK
IS AVAILABLE FROM THE LIBRARY OF CONGRESS

ISBN-13: 978-1-4328-7069-0 (hardcover alk. paper)

Published in 2019 by arrangement with Harper, an imprint of
HarperCollins Publishers

Printed in Mexico
1 2 3 4 5 6 7 23 22 21 20 19

For Steve and Cindy Weir

CHAPTER 1

So many men killed now, fallen to his gun.

But none of them the man he wanted to kill: Ben Trask.

The last three men hadn't needed to die. He'd given them a chance and a choice. Maybe it was something in the outlaw way of thinking. Three against one was fair odds. Maybe they thought they were better than he. Well, they had found out and now they were cold dead meat. Fair odds, fair warning, he thought.

Ben Trask had brutally murdered Zak Cody's father years before. Now, Trask and several other men were headed east on the old stage road, and Zak meant to stop him in his tracks. He had tracked Ben Trask ever since Russell Cody had been murdered, whenever his undercover military duty allowed him the privilege.

When he'd last spotted Ben Trask and the outlaws, the circumstances were not right to make his move. He knew they would stop at the line shack before long, and figured his opportunity would come after they left the shack.

Cody looked over at Colleen O'Hara, situated with the soldiers in a vale not far from the hill where he had stationed himself. She had been hired as a teacher at Fort Bowie, upon her brother's recommendation. But Lieutenant Ted O'Hara had been kidnapped by Trask and his men before she even arrived at the fort. She had been riding to Tucson, accompanied by two soldiers. When their path crossed that of Zak Cody and the two soldiers in their search for Ben Trask, Colleen had insisted on accompanying them.

Now, hunkered down on the side of the hill, Zak held up a silver dollar so the sun caught it just right, and flashed signals up the old stage road. He was out of sight, the hand that held the coin not visible to anyone down below. He hoped the kidnapped lieutenant, riding among his captors, would see the signals and know that help was coming.

Cody moved the coin slightly after each flash, spelling out the words he wanted the prisoner to decipher. There wasn't much time. Soon, the column of outlaws led by

Trask, the man he was hunting, would be passing the hill. Then he would lose the opportunity to send any more signals to the lieutenant.

His hand ached. Pain coursed down his arm in searing rivulets, burning into his muscles, his flesh, as he manipulated the coin. Flick, flick, flick. Flash, flash, flash.

Help soon, wait, be ready, he signaled over and over until the column of men came too close for the signal to be seen beneath the rise of the hill.

He could hear the hooves of the horses hitting the ground with dull thuds. In the west, a group of clouds appeared on the horizon like the sails of distant sailing ships, their underbellies already turning sable against a stretch of desert landscape that was taking on a sepia hue. The sky had been bloodred that morning, telling him that a storm was coming. Until now, he hadn't known from where, but the signs were all there, in the western sky.

He pulled his hand down, stuck the coin back into his pocket. He flexed his arm and fingers until the feeling returned to the tendons and muscles in his right hand. His gun hand. He drew deep breaths and listened to the unintelligible mutterings of the men, the creak of saddle leather and cinches, the plod of hooves, the crackle of iron shoes on sand.

"I hope the lieutenant got the message," he said to himself, his voice so low it wasn't even a whisper. And none near enough to hear it

He had done what he could to prepare the captured soldier for rescue. That would not be soon. He would have to wait for night, or until the black clouds on the horizon swallowed up the sun.

Lieutenant Ted O'Hara didn't know what to make of it, but there was no mistaking the clear signals he had gotten. Who could have sent them? Jeffords? Could be. Tom Jeffords knew the new Morse code and semaphore. A soldier? An Apache? No, not an Apache. Had to be a soldier. But if so, when could he hope to be rescued? The signaler had told him to wait, to expect help. No time specified. Why not now? And if not now, when? A small mirror, not like the ones the army used. Very small, like a piece of glass, or a silver coin. A quarter, or a dollar, maybe. Strange, he thought. But he took the messages to be friendly. Someone was looking out for him.

Although his hands were not tied, O'Hara knew that Jesse Bob Cavins kept a close watch on him. Still, he could make plans for his escape. He could act when the time came. He was sure of that, but meanwhile went over every move he might have to make when that time came.

Trask set a punishing pace as soon as they reached level ground. He figured that Julio Delgado and the other Mexicans would catch up with them. He had no way of knowing that they were already dead. Trask and the others kept looking back, their anxious gazes on the approaching storm, and there was much talk among the men about past storms in this dry part of the country. None of them wanted to be caught out in the open, where the danger of flash floods was great.

The wind built in some secret corner of the universe and brushed against their backs. The white thunderheads in the west had turned coal black, great bulging elephants stampeding across the heavens like some malevolent herd galloping after them, spreading wide, gobbling up blue sky and blotting out the falling sun.

The clouds seemed to be descending on the outlaw band, and although some of the thunderheads were still snow white, their underbellies had begun to darken like the others, as if they had been smudged with light soot. More and more of these clouds filled the sky as the wind built, blowing high, slowly pushing the clouds together. When they all touched, they would blot out the sun and spark lightning discharges that would open the floodgates for a drenching rain.

Trask and his men stopped at one of the line shacks, fed and watered their horses, then moved on the better part of an hour later.

"When we stop for the night, O'Hara," Cavins said to the prisoner, "you're going to be hog-tied again."

"Are we stopping for the night?"

"I don't know," Cavins replied in a sullen tone. He and the other men had begun to darken like the clouds, their faces drawn and somber, their scowls apparent. They were all tired and knew they had a long way to go.

"You aim to stop for the night, Ben?" Hiram Ferguson asked as the shadows began to lengthen and the sun dropped below the clouds in the west. "I see dark skies back there. Goin' to come a hell of a blow."

"We'll stop at the next line shack tomorrow," Trask said.

"If that storm catches us out in the open, we'll be swimmin' our horses."

"We can always go to high ground."

"And get soaked, either way."

"You got a slicker. Put it on when the rain starts."

"Yeah."

As dusk descended on the land, the riders came upon an adobe line shack. To O'Hara's surprise, every man drew his pistol. Trask made hand signs and the riders fanned out and circled the adobe, each of them wary as he motioned for them to approach.

Cavins stuck close to O'Hara.

"You just hold steady there, soldier, until we find out what's what."

"You're the boss," O'Hara said in his meekest tone.

Cavins wore a satisfied smirk on his face.

"Go on inside, Rawlins," Trask ordered, waving his pistol.

Rawlins dismounted and approached the adobe. O'Hara saw that the corral was empty. The horses whickered at the smell of hay and water in the troughs. There was an eerie quiet as Rawlins went inside the small building. He emerged a moment later, pasty-faced.

"Nobody here," he called to Trask. "Nobody alive, anyways."

"All right, men. Feed and water the horses. Let's see what we have here." Trask dismounted and handed his reins to Al Deets.

"They's a mess in there, Ben," Rawlins said. "Looks like animals drug in two men, and what they didn't eat, the worms and buzzards chewed on. Stinks of buzzard and coyote crap inside."

"Tend to your horse, Rawlins," Trask said. He walked up to the door and saw the blood outside, marks of where men had been dragged inside the adobe. He stepped inside.

It was difficult to tell if the bodies inside were human. If they hadn't had pieces of clothing still clinging to their ravaged bodies, he would have been hard put to identify the men.

"Ferguson," he called. "Come on in here."

Ferguson entered a few moments later.

"Recognize these men?" Trask asked.

"Not hardly."

"Take a good look. They yours?"

Ferguson pinched his nose with two fingers and bent over one corpse, backed away, then waddled over to the other. He swore an oath under his breath. He stood up and walked to the door.

"Well?"

14

"Near as I can tell, Ben, that near one used to be Dave Newton. And, t'other one might be Lester Cunningham. Men I had here, all right. Can't tell how they died."

"Well, they didn't die of old age."

"I don't reckon."

Ferguson went outside, followed a moment later by Trask.

"That damned Cody did this," Trask said.

"I don't think a human —"

"I mean he killed those men. I know he didn't eat them, you fool."

"They was good men."

"Not good enough, apparently," Trask said, his anger boiling just below the surface.

He knew that Zak Cody had been there. He felt it in his bones.

There weren't enough curses to use on the bastard, he thought. But he used the vilest that he could summon from memory at that moment.

Trask had never wanted to kill a man as much as he wanted to kill Zak Cody. He had felt his presence in the room. Could almost smell him. The man was like a damned cur dog. He just couldn't get rid of him.

Not yet, anyway. But someday he'd get Cody in his sights and blow him straight to hell.

CHAPTER 2

O'Hara watched Trask and Ferguson step outside the adobe shack. Ferguson looked sick, as if he might throw up. His nose bore the marks of his fingertips where he had pinched it.

Most of the men rolled smokes while their horses drank the murky water or nibbled on hay in the open corral.

O'Hara walked around, stretching his legs. Cavins, like his shadow, traipsed after him.

In the distance he could see streaks of lightning lacing the far black clouds, tracing silver spiderwebs from horizon to horizon as intricate and ephemeral as snowflakes. The sun had set, but there was still a faint greenish glow at the bottom of the sky.

Trask beckoned for all the men to gather around him.

"There's food inside that 'dobe," he said. "Fidel, you and Hector start passing out what we can use. Jaime can help you. We should have more than enough to last us until we get to the next line shack."

"We goin' to ride all night?" Al Deets asked.

"Yeah, we're going to ride all night. Keep your eyes open. We could get jumped any time. I don't expect it, but as long as Cody is riding around somewhere, he might take a pot shot or two when we least expect it."

"You expecting some kind of ambush, boss?" Willy Rawlins asked.

"Look, Cody's just one man. But there were four sets of tracks back there this morning. We don't know who those pecker-woods are or where they went. Just ride tight and stay quick. And don't make a hell of a lot of noise. You hear anything out of the ordinary, you let me know."

Most of the men nodded.

Ted thought he detected a sprig of doubt in Trask's garnish of words. Beneath the bravado, Trask seemed worried about one man, a man named Cody. Could that have been the man who had signaled to him with the small mirror or the silver coin?

"Who in hell is this Cody, anyways?" Lou Grissom asked. "And what did he do in that shack? He kill Lester and Dave all by his-self?"

Ferguson opened his mouth, but Trask cut

17

him off.

"Zak Cody is a cold-blooded killer, Grissom. He dry-gulched those two men. The Injuns call him the Shadow Rider. He's sneaky as a snake. You don't hear him comin' up on you and he shoots you in the back."

Ted straightened up. He had heard of the Shadow Rider. Campfire talk, barracks gossip. But he had also heard about a man named Cody, supposed to be working undercover for President Grant and General Crook. He had always taken the talk as just idle rumors, though. Was that who was out there? Zak Cody? He held some kind of army commission, he had heard, but wasn't in the regular army. That's why he had discounted most of the talk. He had never heard of such a thing.

The Mexicans whispered in Spanish among themselves, but he caught some of the words, like *jinete de sombra*. So even the Mexicans knew about Cody. Remarkable, he thought.

"That's why I'm telling you to be on your guard, you men," Trask said. "Now, get to the grub, Fidel, and the rest of you gather up your horses. We're wasting time here."

"I'd like to see that bastard sneak up on me," Deets said. "I'd give him what for."

18

"Aw, you brag too much, Al," Grissom said. "You ain't never seen the man. That's why you're still alive."

Grissom's comment brought a laugh, but Trask cut it short when he held up his hand.

"No more talk about Cody," he said. "Keep your mind on the road ahead. We've got a lot of miles to go."

The darkness came suddenly, and with the night, the distant rumble of thunder. Lightning flashed in the northwestern sky. An hour later they began to feel the wind at their backs and the night seemed to deepen.

It was still. No coyote called. No night birds sang.

It was as if the world had just stopped, its denizens vanished into nothingness.

And all the men, except Ted, were worried about one thing: the Shadow Rider.

Zak Cody might be out there somewhere, stalking them, waiting for the chance to shoot one of them in the back, like Trask had said.

The Shadow Rider began to loom large in their minds, and the sound of thunder grew louder as the storm came toward them, behind their backs, just like Cody might do.

CHAPTER 3

Somewhere, far away to the west, he thought he heard the faint mutter of thunder. And there was a mechanism in his brain that was ticking like a clock. Each minute that passed meant less distance between him and his quarry.

Zak held up his hand, reined up Nox just as the dusk light began to weaken and fade. He turned and began untying the thongs in back of the cantle. He shook out a black slicker and slipped his arms inside the sleeves.

"If you have slickers, best to put them on now," he told the others. Thunder murmured louder in the distance, as if to underline his words.

Colleen O'Hara pulled a yellow slicker from her saddlebags as her horse sidled up next to Zak's.

"I wish we could have rescued Ted when we saw him," she said. "Do you think we'll find him again?"

"Don't worry. Those men won't stay long at the line shack after they discover the dead bodies. They'll ride on, and I know where they're headed."

Colleen smiled. "I won't be able to see you in that dark slicker when night comes on," she said. "Do you always wear black?"

"I'm partial to it."

Her raincoat made a sound like a heavy wet shirt on a windblown clothesline as she shook it out and began to pull it on over her clothing.

"Is that why they call you the Shadow Rider, Zak?"

"I don't know why people call me that."

"Really?"

"Indians started it. The Lakota, then the Blackfeet, the Cheyenne."

"It fits you somehow. You're quiet. You wear black. You ride a black horse."

Scofield and Rivers, the two soldiers on leave from Fort Bowie, put on their dull gray slickers then rode up to Zak, their faces taking on shadows, their eyes bright in the dwindling light. They knew Cody carried the rank of colonel in the U.S. Army, although he was not required to be in uniform. Zak answered only to his immediate superiors, General George Crook and

President U.S. Grant.

"Sir?" Scofield said. "Where are we going, if I might ask?"

Zak turned in the saddle, pointed to a small hill off to their right.

"Be full dark soon," Zak said. "I figure we've gained on Trask, stand ahead of him. I want you and Rivers to take that ridge there and just wait. The old stage road is just below it."

"What about her?" Scofield asked. "Miss O'Hara, I mean."

"She'll stand out like a lighthouse in that yellow slicker," Zak said. "Best you keep her back a little and between you."

"What do you aim to do, Colonel?" Rivers asked.

"I'm going to ride into them once the rain starts and bring Lieutenant O'Hara back to that spot. Now, I'm going to backtrack and come up behind Trask."

"That sounds mighty dangerous to me," Scofield said. "You're one man against what? A dozen or so? They'll shoot you out of the saddle first time they see you."

"We'll see what that storm does for me," Zak said. "It's heading in from the west, and that bunch won't be looking back much. If there's wind — and I expect there will be — that rain will sting their eyes like blown cactus spines."

He knew he was taking a big risk. But life itself was a big risk, he thought. When a babe was born, that child was at risk until the first breath was taken. After that, it was one risk after another. He had long ago accepted as much; something his pa had told him.

"Life don't hand you nothin', Zak," Russell Cody had said. "If they shoot at you, pick up a gun. If they chase you, run. If it's kill or be killed, you be the killer, else you'll take that last breath and be right back where you started."

Good advice, Zak thought. But General Crook was paying him to put his life on the line.

"You see something wrong, Zak, you fix it before the army's called in," the general had told him. "I'm asking a lot, I know, but no more than you've already given in the service of your country."

Trask had kidnapped a soldier serving in the United States Army. And he was out to stir up trouble among the Chiricahua, who were at peace, at least temporarily. Crook, he thought, would approve of this mission. Especially if he pulled it off and kept the army out of it.

Now they could all see the lightning and

hear the muttering rumble of distant thunder. The air had changed, too, and the wind was picking up, gusting in their faces, rattling the slickers, dislodging small pebbles on the hillside.

"Zak," Colleen said as he touched a forefinger to the brim of his hat and turned Nox to the west. "Please be careful. And bring Ted back with you."

The way her face glowed in the strange dim light made her look like some statues of the Madonna he had seen. There was a radiance in her that made her skin appear soft and silky. He felt a tug in his chest as if an unseen talon had pulled gently at his heart. For a schoolteacher, he thought, she was mighty pretty, and those eyes of hers seemed to bore right through him, in a gentle, caring way. Such thoughts were uncommon to him, and he knew he could not afford to be distracted by them. He tried to shake them off and not look at her inviting lips.

"If you're shot at," Zak said to all three of them, "shoot back."

His voice was sterner than it had to be, he knew, but it was the only way he could override his growing feelings for Colleen O'Hara. She seemed to gather that faint light to her, gray light that she turned into a

24

translucent shade of pearl.

And then he was gone. As the dusky twilight melted into night, the clouds blackened to coal and lowered, as lightning flashed silver warnings in the west. Colleen watched Zak disappear into the darkness and sighed deeply as Scofield and Rivers turned their horses toward the dim hill that rose above a road only Zak had known was there.

Zak knew he had to be some distance ahead of Trask. He figured they would stop at the first line shack, grub up, and then put their horses into a mile-eating canter. He would not have long to wait, he knew.

Nox was tired, and for a while he let the horse walk in his quiet, careful way. He turned toward the road, saw its faint outline, and rode toward a spot where broken hills came together in a jumble. He crossed the road and found the perfect place, a place where he could not be seen when the outlaws rode by.

He hoped the storm would hit before he spotted Trask, but knew it might be tight. Still, the thunder was growing louder and more frequent, and the bursts of lightning gave him glimpses of the road for a good quarter mile or so. The wind stiffened and

Nox bobbed his head at every rattle of rock, every rustle of desert flora. The road was empty.

Fifteen minutes later, Zak felt a dash and a sprinkle of rain. The clouds descended still lower and the wind picked up, steady, with brisk gusts that peppered his eyes with grit, stung the skin on his face. He pulled his hat down tighter on his head, slid his bandanna up from around his neck to cover his face.

Nox lifted his head and turned toward the westering stretch of road, his ears hardening to stiff cones, twitching ever so slightly. Beneath the rumble of thunder, Zak thought he heard hoofbeats. Then a streak of lightning coursed the clouds and exploded into silvery ladders. A second later the crack of thunder told him the storm was less than a mile away.

Rain splashed his face, soaking through the bandanna, and then he was caught in a steady downpour. Lightning threaded the clouds and the thunder boomed. He could hear water starting to run down the little hills, but the ground was dry where he sat his horse. He rummaged in his saddlebag and pulled out the pistol he had taken from one of the men he had killed. He slid it behind his belt so that he could get to it easily when the time came.

The rain streamed down in thick heavy sheets, and visibility dropped to a few measly yards. The sound of hoofbeats faded as if they had never existed, but he knew Trask was coming, riding his way, perhaps more slowly now that the storm had struck.

Zak patted Nox on the neck to calm him and strained his eyes, squinting to keep the rain from stinging them as he gazed hard down the road. He slid the bandanna back down around his collar and felt the icy drip of water stream down his back. He wiped his eyebrows and eyelids with a swipe of his sleeve and dipped his head, water cascading off the brim of his hat like a small watery veil.

The road turned slick, glistened under the lightning flashes, and then began to boil mud as the water soaked into the ground.

The first rider emerged out of the rain, but Zak could not identify him. Then the others plodded into sight. The riders were strung out in a long ragged line. He was looking for one man, and when he saw him, knew what he must do.

Ted O'Hara rode with his head down, another man close behind him but losing ground. Trask had already gone by, holding one hand above his eyebrows to shield his face from the rain. The wind lashed and spattered rain in all directions as it swirled in the teeth of the storm.

Zak eased Nox out of the little box they were in, drifting onto the road so slowly that he hoped the dark shape of horse and man would not be noticed. He mentally pictured himself and Nox as a large shadow.

And that's what he and Nox were, a shadow among shadows.

CHAPTER 4

The rain pelted down hard, as if poured from a giant bucket in the sky. The wind, funneled through rocky hills on both sides of the road, blasted horses and men with a savage ferocity.

As Zak got into line with the outlaw riders, he saw that their heads were bent down. They were looking straight down, their backs hunched like mendicants, not looking around them. He rode at their pace, but tapped Nox's flanks with his spurs, easing gradually up among them until he was riding alongside O'Hara.

Zak stretched a hand to touch Ted on the arm, and the lieutenant turned toward him, head still bowed. Zak squeezed his arm twice then withdrew his hand and gestured for him to follow. To his relief, Ted complied and began to drift toward him.

When Ted was close enough, Zak pulled the Colt from his waist and handed it across to him, and he grabbed it as a drowning man would grasp a hank of driftwood. Ted held the pistol tight against his middle, his thumb on the hammer of the single-action. He looked over at Zak quickly but could not see his face. All he saw was a man dressed in black riding a black horse.

Zak saw an opening in front of Ted, crossed over and began drifting left toward the other side of the slick, muddy road. He looked back and saw that Ted was following him, as he'd hoped the lieutenant would.

Jesse Bob Cavins, who had been riding with head down behind Zak, looked up just then, pointed at Ted and yelled, "The soldier's gettin' away!"

Zak drew his pistol, cocked and aimed it in one smooth motion, then squeezed the trigger. As the gun roared, Cavins reared back in the saddle, clutching his stomach. He gurgled and then his saddle emptied as he fell to the ground.

"Come on, Ted," Zak yelled, already riding toward a gap in the low hills off to his left. He glanced up and saw the yellow raincoat atop the next rise.

The outlaws began yelling and drawing their pistols.

Ted turned and fired at the nearest one, Al Deets. The orange flame from the muzzle of his pistol lit the night and painted his face with a sudden bright flash of orange. Rain fell thick and strong as pistols cracked and bullets whistled over Ted's head. He followed Zak through the narrow gap between hills.

From atop the next hill, Zak heard the sharp reports of the Spencer carbines, and then a short bark that sounded like a pistol; O'Hara's, he guessed. Men screamed and the line of riders broke up and scattered. He picked out a man turning his horse and fired at him, squeezing the trigger of the Walker Colt. The man jerked, then fell from his saddle. His foot caught in one stirrup and the horse dragged his flopping body away.

More shots sounded and bullets whined off sodden rocks next to where Zak and Ted sat their horses. Ted fired at one of the Mexicans and saw him throw up his hands, then slump dead in the saddle.

"Where in hell is Trask?" Zak yelled, his eyes straining to see through the rain and the dark.

"He rode off, I think," Ted yelled across to Zak. "Who's that shooting from up on that ridge?"

"Two soldiers and your sister, Colleen."

"Colleen? She's here?"

Zak didn't answer. Another man made a dash toward them, his six-gun barking, orange flame spewing from the barrel.

"Too bad you didn't follow your boss," Zak said, then dropped him with a single shot. The man tumbled out of the saddle and landed with a splash in a puddle of water.

Zak took off again, pushing Nox up the steep hill and toward the ridge on top. He heard the faint pounding of hoofbeats as the riders fled, leaving their dead behind. He listened to the rain and the wind, then wiped his eyes. He surprised Ted when he turned around and abruptly stopped. He reached into his saddlebag, pulled out a bundle and handed it to Ted.

"Put this on when you have a chance."

Ted looked down at the bundle in his hands. It was his own shirt. The bars on the shoulders lit up with a flash of lightning. He stuffed the shirt inside his raincoat.

Zak eyed the road below, making sure that Trask's men were indeed riding away.

When he turned around, Ted had his slicker off and was removing the shirt his captors had given him. He tossed the shirt to the ground, put on his regulation shirt, then slipped back into his soogan.

"Let's go find your sister," Zak said, the

wind whipping the words from his mouth.

Moments later, Ted and Zak were on top of the hill. Colleen ran up to them, slipping a pistol back into her waistband. She held out her arms and collapsed in her brother's arms when he dismounted, and he hugged her tightly as Scofield and Rivers watched.

"They run like rabbits," Rivers said, looking down at the road.

"Plumb gone, lickety-split," Scofield said, grinning.

"I wonder if either of you got a shot at Ben Trask," Zak said.

"He the one who lit out first?" Rivers said.

"I think so. He might have been."

"Lit a shuck before we could level on him," Scofield said. "But I think we might have dropped one or two apiece. It was like a turkey shoot there for a minute or two."

"We need to know who we got," Zak said. "Ted, I might need you to identify some of them."

"I know you hit Cavins with your first shot," Ted said. "I saw him go down, but I don't know if he's dead. He was still squirming around on the ground, last I saw him. You Cody?"

"Yes. Zak Cody."

The two men shook hands, their faces glistening with rain.

Colleen smiled. "I'm so grateful to you, Zak —"

"Don't mention it," Zak said before she could finish.

All he could think about just then was that Trask was getting away. As long as he was alive, Zak would not rest. He would pursue him to the ends of the earth if need be. It was army business now, of course, but it was still personal, too.

"We going down to look at the dead, Colonel?" Scofield asked.

A bolt of lightning struck nearby. The smell of it filled the air with crackling ozone.

"We'll stay up here on high ground until this storm passes," Zak said. "We go down there, we could drown."

"Maybe that Trask feller will get caught in a flash flood and drown hisself," Rivers said.

Zak didn't say anything. He looked at Colleen, who was hanging onto her brother's arm. He took in a deep breath, let the air out slow.

He might have been a bit jealous if Ted hadn't been her brother.

Maybe he was anyway.

A woman like that could get to a man.

He was sure she already had.

He turned away, put his back to the rain and listened to its dancing song, the drumming thunder in the background. There was so much he wanted to say to Colleen. But now was not the time and this was definitely not the place.

But there would be another day, and until then, time to think.

Time to think about so many things.

CHAPTER 5

Lightning stitched latticework across the sky, scratched out trees of silver in the black clouds. The rain drove at them in slanted lances, blown by the hard wind, as they huddled on the ridge. The night was as dark as the depths of a coal mine, and the desert had turned cold.

Zak Cody shaded his eyes, peered down into the gully below and the road beyond it. With the next flash of lightning, he saw that the gully was empty, except for the bodies of two dead men awash in a muddy torrent.

The wind swept across the top of the ridge as Cody bent over, his back to the pelting rain, and reloaded his Colt pistol. The two soldiers, Delbert Scofield and Hugo Rivers, tried to shield Colleen O'Hara and her brother Ted.

"We've got to get off this ridge," Cody yelled into the teeth of the wind. "Follow me. Lieutenant, lead your horse down behind me."

"Call me Ted, will you?"

Cody didn't answer.

"What about Trask and Ferguson, that band of cutthroats?" Ted said, his mouth close to Cody's ear.

"Long gone. By now they're probably in a line shack, out of the weather. I'm more concerned about somebody else right now."

"Who?" O'Hara asked.

"Three Mexicans. Part of Trask's bunch. They stayed behind to bury a woman. They ought to be up this way about now."

"You mean . . . ?"

"I mean we've got to keep an eye on our back trail."

"Hard to do. In this storm, I'm lucky if I can see ten feet ahead."

"There are other ways to see," Zak said cryptically.

Ted looked over his shoulder. Needles of rain stung his eyes and he had to close them and turn his head out of the wind. With a sinking feeling, as if his whole body were subsiding into quicksand, he realized they were all pretty much defenseless against anyone riding up behind them.

"Let's go," Zak said, loud enough for all of them to hear.

Nox, his black horse, stood hipshot, his

hindquarters blasted by wind and rain. He raised his head as Cody took the reins and started down the backside of the ridge.

"I don't think I can find my horse," Scofield said. He and Rivers had left the horses below before climbing the ridge with Colleen earlier, to give Cody cover when he'd gone after Ted O'Hara. "I hope they ain't run off."

Cody said nothing. He held onto Colleen's hand, and she held onto her brother's, as the small group inched their way down a rock-strewn slope running with rivulets of water. The footing was slippery, treacherous.

The wind wasn't as strong at the foot of the ridge, but Zak knew they'd find no relief until they got to the other side of the hump. First, though, they had to find the horses Colleen and the soldiers had left on the flat.

Lightning strikes danced across the empty desert, illuminating a desolate landscape a split second at a time. It was like living in a nightmare, Zak thought. The sound of thunder rolled across the skies as if it had come from a thousand cannons, a thousand throats of unearthly demons on a rampage.

How many men will I have to kill to get to Ben Trask? he asked himself, to drown out the sound of pealing thunder in his head. He had already killed too many, and now the storm had allowed Trask to elude him. For a time. Trask could not know that the men he had left in shacks along the old stage road would not be able to help him. They were all dead. All had fallen to the snarl and roar of his gun. They were help that Trask was never going to get. But Trask would go on. He was bent on finding the Apache gold he believed Cochise had hidden. Trask was not only a stone cold killer, he was a fool.

Zak heard the low whicker of one of the horses, and led the others to them. Sheets of rain lashed them as they climbed into their saddles.

Zak climbed onto Nox and rode over to the lieutenant.

"Ted, just follow the edge of this hill to the end. You might find some shelter on the other side, near the road."

"Where are you going?" Ted asked.

"I'm going to get the gun rig off of Cavins. You might need another sidearm. I'll join up with you in a while."

"How long's this rain going to last?"

"All night, probably. Just sit tight when you find shelter. Wait for me."

Zak turned his horse, then was gone.

"Sis," Ted said to Colleen. "Who in hell is

that man?"

"Nobody knows, really," she said, her voice soft, a wistful note in it.

"Can we trust him?"

"He saved your life, didn't he?"

"Yes, but —"

"Ever hear of the Shadow Rider, Ted?"

Ted didn't say anything for a long moment. His face was wet with rain. Colleen looked like a drenched bird. The two soldiers waited, their backs bowed, their heads lowered against the wind and the whipping curtains of rain.

"Not much. The men who captured me were talking about it, and I've heard talk of such a man around the fort. Ex-army. Something to do with General Crook."

"Well, that's him. Zak Cody. He's a strange man."

"But you like him, don't you?"

"I'm not sure," she said. "He . . . He's magnetic. He's not my type, but —"

"Admit it, you like him, sis."

"Shouldn't we get out of this rain, Ted? Zak put you in charge."

"Seems to me," Ted said, "that your friend Zak's in charge."

Ted dug spurs into his horse's flanks. They moved along the base of the ridge, the wind at their backs.

"Yes," she said. "I'd say you were right, Ted. From what I hear, Zak is, or was, a colonel in the army. That's what the two army men were calling him. I don't know why he's here, but I'm glad he is."

"Well, I'm damned sure going to find out who I'm riding with. Even if he did save my life. He took a hell of a risk, now that I think of it. We both could have been shot."

Colleen said nothing. She was thinking about Zak and her feelings for him. They were all tangled up, like vines in the trellis of her mind. She could not sort them out, now that he was gone into the night and the rain, after having thought of her brother, not of himself. And he'd said there might be more men coming up the road. He could be riding straight back into danger.

She shuddered at the thought, and the vines began to straighten and line up, a string of green leaves bright with energy and promise.

CHAPTER 6

Lieutenant Ted O'Hara took charge. He struck out along the base of the ridge, as Cody had instructed him, with Colleen, Scofield, and Rivers following him. It was pitch-black, raining and blowing hard. There were no other reference points along the route, no trail to follow. But he had no difficulty keeping to the left of the baseline.

His mind reeled with thoughts of Zak Cody and the fight on the old stage road. Cody had been very brave to attack as he had, in the dark, badly outnumbered. He had deployed Scofield and Rivers wisely, stationing them on the top of that ridge, and Colleen had been part of it, too, providing still another rifle. His sister was a good shot. Their father had taught them well. But he was still in the dark about all of it. Where had Cody come from, and why? Was he in the army, following orders? He didn't know. He had a lot of questions and no answers.

Ted didn't mind being out in the weather. He had been cooped up as a prisoner for so long he welcomed the good air, even if it tasted like metal as lightning etched quicksilver hieroglyphs across the elephantine sky while thunder boomed like empty barrels rolling across an attic floor. He had been out, away from the fort so long — tracking Cochise and other Apache bands, sitting with them, giving them tobacco, smoking with them, eating with them — that he had lost his relish for barracks roofs and adobe walls.

He wondered what Cochise and his tribe were doing just then. From what he knew of the Apache, they would view the storm much differently than the white man did. To them, the thunder would be the voice of God, the Great Spirit, and the lightning a demonstration of power — immense power over all things. They would see the thunderbolts as arrows and lances shot and hurled from on high, striking game or humans who were not pure, setting fires, burning rocks and sand with a force no mortal man could match. He wondered now if he had gotten too close to the Apache. Was he beginning to think like they did?

One day, when he had returned from Cochise's camp to the place where his patrol was bivouacked, his sergeant, Ronnie Casteel, asked him that same question in another way.

"Lieutenant O'Hara, sir, do you think you might be spendin' too much time palaverin' with them Apaches?"

"What do you mean, Ronnie?"

"You never stayed away all night before. We was worried."

"I was perfectly safe."

"At night, when you sleep, the men can hear you talkin' that gibberish what you talk with them Apaches."

"That gibberish is Spanish, Sergeant."

"Well, the men are just wonderin' if you are turnin' into a squaw man."

"What's a squaw man?"

"More Injun than white."

"I assure you, Ronnie, I've still got the same blood. I might add that it's no different than yours or Cochise's, for that matter. I speak Spanish with Cochise because I can't speak Apache. He speaks Spanish — Mexican, really — so we can converse. It's essential that I know what he's thinking. Our conversations help me to know what's on Cochise's mind."

"Why should you care what that old bird is thinkin'?"

"Because we're here to keep the peace

with the Chiricahuas, and to calm the fears of the white settlers. That good enough for you, Ronnie?"

"Sir, I didn't mean no disrespect."

"Of course you didn't. But if you're talking about respect, it wouldn't hurt to show some to the Apaches. We're in their country, after all."

"We are? I thought we was in the United States."

"The Apaches don't have the same feelings about land that we do. We whites, I mean. They believe that land is a gift from God, the Great Spirit, and they don't abide ownership, by any man or tribe, red or white."

"That ain't practical, sir."

Ted didn't argue any further, but now, that conversation came back to him, and he thought of how he felt looking at land and the ownership of land through the eyes of the Chiricahua. When he was out there, with his men or with the Apaches, he felt unfettered, free. When he lay on his bedroll at night and looked up at the stars, looking so bright and close, he thought the heavens were surely a part of it all, part of some grand scheme bestowed on man by a higher intelligence, a God, if that be the belief, or a Great Spirit, as the Apaches believed.

No man could own a star, or a bunch of stars, or a planet, the sun, or the moon. Why should it not be the same for the land on planet Earth? Sometimes he thought the Apaches made more sense than those of his own skin color and descendents. Boundaries, he thought, kept people apart. Ownership created enemies, foes that would kill to possess an acre or a section, a township or a great metropolis. And at the heart of it all was greed, the same greed that he saw in Ferguson and Trask. Trask believed that Cochise had a great golden treasure, and he was determined to possess it. And both he and Ferguson and their men would gladly kill to get it.

Among the Apaches he had known, he had seen no signs of greed or envy, and the revelation was a puzzle to him. The white men he had known, his own kind, coveted things — land, wealth, women — and none considered the cost of acquisition, but sought and strived for things they did not possess. While the Apaches were grateful for what they had, a wealth no white man could fathom, the earth, the sky, water, and, most valuable of all, friends and family. Gifts, they said, from a spirit so strong it gave them strong hearts and invaded their dreams, opened their eyes to all the wonders of the heaven and the hidden riches of the earth: food and shelter and clothing, and vistas so wondrous they painted the horizon at sunset and dawn.

They reached the butt of the ridge and Ted turned his horse, rounding the corner. His sister and the two soldiers followed after him. He noticed a decided drop in the wind. There, in the lee of the butte, or whatever it was, the rain no longer drove into them with the force of war arrows. It was still wet and rainy, but at least they were out of the wind.

"Dismount," he ordered, "and gather the horses close, bunch 'em up. We'll squat under them and maybe not get any wetter."

"Good idea, sir," Rivers said.

A bolt of lightning speared the ground nearby, atop the next hill, and thunder roared from above a moment later. The air smelled of burnt mercury and tasted faintly of iodine or copper. Colleen ducked and shivered as she brought her horse in close to the others.

They huddled together beneath their horses, exchanging the heat of their bodies with their breaths and the pulsing of the blood in their veins. The horses' bellies, too, gave off warmth and provided shelter from the pelting rain. The wind streamed past them on both sides of the hill, but whipped back now and then to lash them, draw them closer together as if they were bound together by something like the string of a purse.

"That wind's a blue one, all right," Scofield said, his teeth clacking together like dice in a tin cup.

"What I wouldn't give to be back in the barracks," Rivers said.

"If you don't think of it so much," O'Hara said, "you won't feel it so bad. Isn't that right, Colleen?"

"I think of warm zephyrs and a fire in the hearth," she said, her voice quavering from the cold, the bone-penetrating chill.

"I c-c-can't think of nothing else but the cold with that wind howlin' like a banshee," Scofield said.

"I'm thinkin' about that Cody feller," Rivers said. "He's out in it by hisself, huntin' men like they was meat."

"Yeah," Scofield said. "He be a strange one, all right."

O'Hara thought of Cody and how he had ridden into the outlaw column, all alone, and rescued him, against all odds.

"What do you think of him, Lieutenant?" Rivers asked.

"I don't know what to make of him. He's uncommon brave. I know that."

Colleen said nothing. She was thinking of Zak Cody, too, wondering why he was not with them. Was he brave or foolhardy? What could he see in the dark and the rain? Was he protecting them, or did he just thirst for blood? She did not like to think of the latter possibility. But was she just projecting him onto her mind in a fabricated image, making him into someone she wanted him to be, denying to herself who he really was? She knew she was responding to his magnetism. She felt the pull of his gravity, and it was disturbing to her, like certain dreams she'd had that she could not fathom.

No one spoke for a few moments, each locked in their own private thoughts of Zak Cody, perhaps wondering what he was doing out in the weather while they crouched like drenched birds beneath their horses, waterfalls cascading from their saddles, rain trickling down quivering legs, pooling up in hoofprints, sputtering under the onslaught of dancing raindrops.

They heard a sound then. The wind carried it through the liquid crystal curtains of showers, carried it, muffled it, and spewed it to their ears like a dissonant crackle escaped from a long forgotten thunder. They stiffened as if each had been larruped with the lash of a bullwhip. The sound was unmistakable, oddly disconnected from the storm, but part of it as well.

A gunshot that seemed to speak of fire and blood, the violence that sprouted from a dark wet world while the sky bristled with branches fashioned of mercury and quicksilver, as if conjured by some ancient alchemist risen from the underworld.

CHAPTER 7

Ben Trask had been watching the darkening sky and knew the fierce storm was coming toward them. He and his men put their horses through a punishing pace, hoping to reach the next line shack before the rain and wind hit them.

It was already dark by the time Trask spotted the adobe. And the rain had already started to fall. He rode up to the front of the shack, whose door was ajar, and motioned for the other men to follow him.

Just then, a crack of lighting lit the scene. It was followed almost immediately by thunder, which pealed across the sky like a battery of twelve-pounders. At the same time, rain sloshed down like an engulfing tidal wave, the horses screamed terrified whinnies, and the men jerked their reins to hold them, so they wouldn't bolt out from under them.

Trask yelled into the explosive downpour,

"Everybody inside. We got a gusher. Tie up your horses on high ground." The men dismounted and struggled through the wind and the rain as if they were slogging through quicksand. Some shook out lariats and led their horses out in back of the adobe. They tied their mounts to anything solid they could find as the rain continued to drench them. The wind tore at their soaked clothing, stung their faces. They put hobbles on some of the horses and tied these animals to the secured mounts and fled to the front of the shack to get in out of the rain.

Trask was the first one in the door. He couldn't see at all in the darkness. He held his arms out in front of him, as a blind man might do, feeling for anything that might be in his path. He took two steps into the room and tripped over something on the floor.

"Damn," he said, regaining his balance in time to keep from falling down. A streak of lightning lit the inside of the adobe just long enough for Trask to see what he'd stumbled over. It was a body, and he got a glimpse of another corpse on the floor a few feet away. He knew they were men who worked for Hiram Ferguson.

Trask barked at Fidel and Hector Gonzalez, "Haul them bodies outside, toss 'em on the road. Flood's going to take 'em away right soon."

The other Mexicans, followed by Ferguson, poured into the adobe and helped remove the dead bodies.

The adobe sat on high ground above the road, but Trask worried that they might not be high enough. He knew what was coming. So did Ferguson, who walked over to Trask, his wet face the color of cork. With the constant strikes of lightning, Ferguson could see the fear flickering in Trask's dilated eyes like restless shadows.

"Gonna come a flash flood, Ben, sure as shootin'."

"It's a frog strangler, all right," Trask said.

Fidel and Hector bent down to pick up one of the bodies. It had been ripped and torn by animals — coyotes, possibly — and they struggled with the feet and shoulders. They turned their heads as if to avoid the stench and stood up. Trask cleared a path for them. Rain shot through the door almost in straight lines as the two men stumbled outside.

"Get that other man out of here," Trask ordered, looking at Jaime Elizondo. Pablo, you help him," he said to Pablo Medina.

The two men went over to the other body, which was in worse shape than the first. It was hardly recognizable as being human.

One leg was completely gone, the other reduced to blood-smeared bone. The face was gnawed off and there was only a skull under the matted hair. They slid their arms under the dead man's back and hefted him up. He wasn't heavy because there wasn't much left of him. They walked outside, ducking to avoid the stinging needles of rain, and sloshed off into the darkness.

Willy Rawlins turned away from the hideous sight. He doubled over and started to retch, but clamped a hand to his mouth and held on, breathing air through his nostrils. As was typical of the adobes, there was no glass covering the windows, which were more like gaping holes than windows. He stepped close to one of them and stood up straight, gulping in fresh wet air. He swore and shook his head as if to clear it of the smells of decaying flesh, coyote dung, urine, and a dozen other scents he could not identify.

"Christ," Ferguson said.

"Get used to it," Trask said, a note of contempt in his voice. "It ain't goin' to get no better."

The adobe seemed to shudder with the next crack of thunder. Lightning flashed all around, limning the windows and the doorway with a flood of bright light. The wind blew rain through every opening.

"Rawlins, close that damned door," Trask said, and Rawlins started to close it when Hector and Fidel dashed back in, their slickers bright with rain. He closed the door, and moments later the other two men opened it and came in. The wind took the door and slammed it into the adobe. Rawlins had to step outside and fight the wind to close it again. The blasts of air and rain made the door rattle and creak, but it stayed closed, pinned shut by the wind.

"Any of you boys want to catch some shut-eye, there's a bunk yonder, or you can get your bedrolls and bring 'em in here," Trask said. "I want at least three men on watch. You can take turns, starting now."

"I'll take the first watch," Rawlins said. "Shit, I'm soakin' wet. Can we make a fire in here?"

"No," Trask said. "I don't want no light showin'."

Rawlins grumbled, but took up a position next to a front window where he would stand watch.

Ferguson pointed to Jaime Elizondo and Fidel Gonzalez. "You two stand first watch," he said. "I'll relieve you, Jaime, in three hours."

Jaime nodded and stood at another window.

Gonzalez took up a position at the back window.

"Can somebody go back out there and get our bedrolls?" Lou Grissom said. Nobody answered. "I'll go, then. Who all wants their bedrolls?"

Everyone answered in the affirmative.

"Take me two trips, likely," Grissom said. "You bunch of yellow-bellied cowards."

Some of the men laughed.

He want out into the rain and closed the door behind him without being asked.

"Too bad we lost that soldier, O'Hara," Ferguson said to Trask. "And I reckon that Cody kilt Cavins and Deets."

"Looks like," Trask said. "We don't need O'Hara. I've got the maps he marked up for us. We can find Cochise's gold without him."

"You think he marked the maps right, Ben?"

"Why not? Hiram, you worry too damned much."

"I worry that those maps might take us right into a trap."

"What makes you think that?" It was turning cold, and Trask shook with a sudden chill.

"I do not trust a soldier to tell the truth

to an enemy," Hiram said. "They are trained to lie."

"Maps don't lie. We know Cochise has a camp somewhere on those maps. We will find him. We will find the damned gold."

"We have lost many men. Cavins and Deets, probably. That shooting back there. They were guarding the lieutenant and now they are not here. And two men dead in this adobe. What about the others?"

"What others?" Trask said.

"The men I had in the other old shacks up the road."

"We'll cross that bridge when we come to it. Take it easy, Hiram. Worry don't get you nowhere. It gets you a damned bellyache."

"I bet that Cody killed all my men on this old road. And we need them if we're going up against the Apache."

"We have enough," Trask said. "If I quit every time the horse bucked, I'd never get anywhere."

"You're stubborn," Ferguson said. "Stubborn as a dadgummed army mule."

"Can we smoke, boss?" Rawlins said.

"No. No lights. And no talkin' from here on."

"Hell, who's gonna hear us talk in this racket?" Rawlins said, referring to the rain slapping the adobe and the rumble of thunder, which was almost constant.

Rawlins couldn't see the glare that flared in Trask's eyes, but he could feel something burn on his cheek and knew Trask was looking at him. He shifted the weight on his feet and said nothing as he turned back to stare out the window at the slashing rain that beat at the door with an erratic, windblown tattoo.

Trask admitted to himself that he was stubborn, but he gave the trait credit for keeping him alive all these years. The West was a savage place, more dangerous than the eastern settlements with their governors and laws. The wildness suited him, though. He often wondered if there was something in the water of a mountain stream that made his blood run hot when he was chasing a man down to rob him, or a man was chasing him. Ever since he had killed Cody's father, robbed him of his gold, he knew that he was a savage man at heart, and he exulted in that knowledge, as he exulted in the savagery of the West itself. In some ways, he admired the red man because an Indian lived by his wits, often with nothing more than a war club, a bow, and arrows. He had no use for them as people but admired the hot blood that ran in their veins. He had taken his share of scalps just so he would know what it felt like, and the feeling he got from taking a life was like a drink of the strongest whiskey mixed with the blackest, hottest, strongest coffee. The feeling burned all through him at such times, and it lingered in his memory like banked coals, always there, basking, glowing, ready to take flame from breath or the wave of a hand.

Lightning danced in the dark sky, dashing their faces with phosphorous. Strikes landed close by and the air smelled of sulfur. With each whip crack of sound, the thunder boomed and the adobe seemed to shake with the fury of the storm. The rain fell faster and harder, and the wind whipped and surged with a powerful energy that blew rain through every crack. Each gust made the drops sound like lead pellets hitting the adobe clay like birdshot.

Rawlins shouted above the roar. "Listen."

They all heard it, and some of the men crowded to the window. Trask stood on tiptoes to look out, while Ferguson struggled to see through the mass of men.

The sound was eerie, far off at first, but all recognized it for what it was.

A river was roaring down the road like a locomotive on a downhill run. A mighty sound of water, a wall of water, clogged their ears and struck fear deep into their bowels.

Ferguson swore.

The rushing water muffled his oath and swallowed it up as the flood burst into view. The sound became deafening as tons of water flowed over the road and surged up the slope toward the adobe.

Maybe, Trask thought, the flash flood would catch Cody out in the open and drown him like a rat.

At the same time, he prayed that the water would not rise up to the roof and burst through the windows and door, suffocating them under a deluge of adobe mud.

CHAPTER 8

Zak had to ride to the end of the small butte and around it, then head back up the road to the spot where he had rescued O'Hara. Lightning lit his way, the jagged streaks some distance away but moving closer. He counted off the seconds it took for the sound of thunder to reach him. Six miles, he judged, from the last brilliant burst of lightning until the first thunderclap resounded in his ears.

One slow second of time equaled a mile in distance that the sound traveled. Six seconds, six miles. Not much time, he thought, to encircle the butte, get a rifle and scabbard, ammunition, whatever else he could find that would help him arm O'Hara and feed them all for what promised to be a long and tiring journey.

As he rounded the end of the hill, Zak worried about the storm passing over him and breaking over hard ground that sloped down the road. A flash flood could wash over him, Colleen, O'Hara, and the two soldiers, perhaps drowning them all.

A bolt of lightning speared the ground five hundred yards ahead of him. In the brilliant dazzle, Zak saw a curtain of rain that shimmered like a silver curtain. The thunder followed a second later, and he knew the massive black clouds were going to dump gallons of rain on him before he got to his destination. He touched spurs to Nox's flanks and put the horse into a trot, hoping the animal would not step into a gopher hole and break its leg.

Just before he reached the place where he would turn and head for the road, a gust of wind nearly blew him out of the saddle. It was a straight-line wind that dashed him with gallons of water, so much that he had to hold his breath and breathe through his nose. Then the gust turned into a gale that pressed against his chest and bowed Nox's head.

He rode into the brunt of the lashing front edge of the storm. Out in the open, the wind hit him full force. The rain stung his face with a thousand sharp needles, battered the brim of his hat, spattered against his slicker like steady rounds of grapeshot. Nox fought against the wind, moving his head from side to side, his neck bowed, his eyes barely open, hooded to avoid the stings.

Zak turned the corner of the hill, and Nox wanted to turn tail and head the other way to keep the wind at his rump. He urged the horse on. They found the road, which was already awash, and turned east. Now he had the wind at his back, but there was dangerous lightning all around and Nox was a handful, fighting against instinct and common sense under the annoying dig of his spurs in both flanks. The wind howled up the road, channeled on both sides by high rocky ground.

"Come on, Nox, old boy. Stay with me, son," Zak said, leaning over the pommel, his voice carrying to the horse's ears. He patted Nox's neck to reassure him. "We both could use a good dry barn or a stable."

The darkness was deep, and only the lightning lit their way to the place where Zak had used his pistol against Trask's men. He kept looking for a loose horse, hoping at least one was still there and not galloping off to high ground seeking shelter.

Water began to wash rocks and dirt down the slopes. Zak could hear the flow of water, the clack of rocks against one another, the rushing sound the liquid made as it coursed downhill. He knew the danger. If there were any large rocks above him, they could be dislodged and start a small avalanche, or even just crash into him, smashing him and Nox to the ground, perhaps breaking their bones. He stayed to the center of the road, peering into the blackness, scanning both sides at every sizzle of light from the electrified sky.

At last he saw a dark shape off to his right. He caught just a bare glimpse of something large enough to be a horse and his heart soared in his chest.

"Almost there, Nox," Zak said, and patted his horse's withers.

Another bolt of lightning touched off more thunder and more rain, but he saw the horse, its butt to the wind, its head hanging down, unaware of his presence. Rain had slicked its hide, and when the lightning struck the hilltop off to his right, the light sorrel looked like a metal sculpture, frozen for a moment in the flash, as if some photographer had touched off a tray of flash powder.

Zak headed for the horse. He eased Nox up alongside it and grabbed the trailing reins. The horse did not shy away, but held fast. Zak saw the rifle jutting out of the scabbard on the opposite side. That was enough for him. He would lead the horse to where O'Hara, Colleen, and the two soldiers were waiting and strip the animal there. Perhaps there was grub in the saddlebags. The storm was too heavy to dawdle. All he had to do was ride up the road to the end of the hill on his left and he knew he'd find them waiting for him. He wanted to get out of that false canyon quick in case the rain caused a flash flood before he could reach the folks he had sent on ahead.

As Zak started up the road, he heard a voice on the opposite side.

"You hold on there. That's my horse."

"Who are you?" Zak asked, trying to find the source of the voice. The darkness hid the man who had called out to him.

"I'm Jesse Bob Cavins. Who are you? Al? That you? Deets, I — I got plugged."

Zak wondered if it was one of the men he had shot. Probably, he thought.

If so, he hadn't killed him. But how badly was the man wounded?

"Yeah, Jesse Bob. It's me, Al," Zak lied. "Tell me where you are."

"That really you, Deets?" Cavins said.

Zak saw him then, a shadowy hulk against the bank. Crippled, but still alive and standing on his feet. Slouching was more like it.

"Yeah," Zak said. "Put away that pistol, will you?"

"You sound funny, Al," Cavins said.

"The rain."

"Yeah, the wind, too."

Cavins moved, and Zak saw that he was holstering his pistol. He nudged spurs into Nox's flanks and the horse approached Cavins with wariness, sidestepping toward him as if ready to bolt. Zak pulled on the reins so Nox felt the bit against his tongue and mouth.

A flash of lightning illuminated Cavins. Zak saw the darker stains on his slicker, streaks that were being washed away. There was a lot of blood. He figured he must have caught Cavins in the gut or just below the ribs.

The lightning revealed Zak to Cavins as well.

"You ain't Al Deets," Cavins said, his voice a throaty rasp.

"You figured that out, did you?" Zak said.

"Damn it, who in hell are you? Trask send you back for me?"

"In a way, yeah."

"Well, help me get on my horse, then."

"I'm taking your horse, Cavins."

"You what?"

"You won't need your horse anymore. And you've seen your last sunrise."

"Damn you. You ain't with Trask."

"No, I'm not."

"Who in hell are you?"

"I'm the man who put that bullet in your gut, Cavins."

The wind whipped up the road, dashed rain like flung sand on both men. Streaks of jagged lightning etched the black clouds with silver filigree, and the ensuing thunder belched in a mighty basso profundo that reverberated across the stormy skies like some dire pronouncement from an Olympian deity.

Cavins jumped when the thunder roared. Then he started to lower his hand in a furtive movement, a slow glide toward his holstered pistol.

"You might want to think twice before you draw that pistol, Cavins," Zak said.

Cavins let his hand float a few inches above the butt of his pistol. It hovered there in midair.

"How's that?" Cavins said, his voice a fear-laden rasp.

"You're looking right up at a big old boulder perched atop a mountain."

"I don't get your meanin', mister."

"I mean you're a raindrop, Cavins. I'm just teetering, waiting for that one drop to dislodge me. Then I'm going to roll down and fall right on top of you."

"You're full of shit," Cavins said, and dropped his hand. He started to pull the pistol from its holster. He might have gotten it going an inch or so when Zak's hand flew to his Walker Colt. Cavins's eyes widened as if the wind had thrown acid into them.

Zak's hand was a blur, and Cavins heard the ominous click as Zak thumbed the hammer back to full cock.

"No," Cavins gasped.

"Yes," Zak said, aiming the pistol straight at Cavins's forehead.

He squeezed the trigger and orange-red flame belched from the muzzle of the Colt. The bullet struck Cavins square between the eyes, smashing bone and flesh to pulp, flattening slightly before it sped through his brain, smashing his head backward into the rocky slope of the hill. His arm and hand went slack and he slid down into a puddle of water, leaving a red streak that turned pink in the rain and then vanished like the bloom on a December rose.

Zak ejected the empty hull from the cylinder of his pistol, shoved a fresh cartridge in, closed the gate, and slid the weapon back in its holster.

Cavins lay sprawled on the ground like a broken doll, his mouth open, eyes fixed in a frosty stare, somehow looking alive as raindrops struck them. In the next lightning flash, Zak saw the black hole in the center of his forehead, washed clean by the rain.

It felt like a graveyard in that spot, so dark and dank and lifeless. He turned Nox away and headed up the road. Cavins's horse trotted after him, his head down, soaked to the skin beneath his hide.

Lightning danced in the skies and thunder rumbled loud and far in the darkness of the night. The wind blew the rain parallel to the earth, a billion stinging needles stabbing the horses, stinging the back of Zak's neck.

Zak hunched over and pulled the collar of his slicker up at the back.

Maybe this was how it was with Noah just after he climbed into the ark, he thought. It felt like the end of the world, and he knew it wouldn't be long before there was a flood somewhere out there on that godforsaken desert where no signs of life were to be seen.

CHAPTER 9

Lieutenant O'Hara saw it first.

A shadow in the rain, looming out of the darkness.

He reached for his pistol with his right hand, touched Colleen's arm with the left. He felt her stiffen.

"Don't shoot," Zak said. "It's me."

The shadow moved toward the clutch of horses, the people huddled beneath them.

"It's only Zak, Ted," Colleen said.

"There's two of 'em," Rivers said.

"Naw, that other shadow's just a horse," Scofield said.

Ted crabbed out from under his horse and stood up, rain pouring over his hat and slicker.

"What you got, Cody?" he asked.

"A rifle for you. Maybe some ammunition in the saddlebags, and grub. You can either change horses or unstrap the rifle and scabbard, switch it to your saddle."

"I'll change horses. Where we going?"

"High ground," Zak said. "This gusher's going to spawn flash floods."

"Right," O'Hara said. "Come on, soldiers, mount up. Colleen, bring my horse to me once I mount the other one."

He walked to the horse Zak was leading and took the reins from him. He climbed into the saddle as the others mounted up.

Colleen led Ted's horse to him and handed him the reins.

"You lead off, Cody," O'Hara said. "This is a fair mount for a civilian horse."

The two soldiers chuckled as Zak pulled away from them on Nox.

He wanted to gain ground on Trask, but he also knew they were all in danger as long as they were on flat ground, at the mercy of the heavy rains. The wind was at their backs, at least, but in such a storm it could circle and come at them head on, slowing them down. It was so dark he could not see very far ahead, but he had been down that old wagon road and he knew there were places where they could get to higher ground. But he might have to range wide of the road to find a suitable place. And wherever they wound up, they'd be at the mercy of the weather, with no trees, no shelter at all.

Lightning ripped through the clouds,

splashed light on the bleak terrain. Thunder was a constant artillery barrage, sometimes so close it was deafening, and off in the distance more thunder and more lightning.

A rattlesnake skittered out in front of Nox, slithering away from the road, its diamond-back skin illuminated briefly from a flash of lightning. It disappeared in the dark, heading, Zak thought, to safer ground, probably flooded out of its home tunnel.

"Follow the snake," he said to himself.

He turned Nox in that direction, marking the path in his mind. The snake would know where to go. Zak could only take his bearings in those brief moments when the land was lighted. He would have to keep all the information in his mind, and all of it in the proper order. The storm would not last forever, and when it was over and the sun came out, he didn't want to be lost.

He didn't know how far ahead of him Trask was, but he had a hunch that the man would be holed up in one of the old stage stops, out of the rain and the wind.

He could not tell, in the darkness, whether the land was rising, but during the next splash of lightning, he saw a low hill off to his right. Was it high enough and wide enough to keep them all safe from any flooding? He did not know, but headed for the hill, and when Nox balked, he kept the horse on course. The horse's hooves dug for purchase, dislodging small stones, sliding some on the wet ground. Zak was conscious of the others behind him, although he could not see or hear them above the roar of thunder.

Nox reached the top of the hill, and as he stepped forward, the ground beneath them leveled. The hill was larger than it had looked. The next lightning strike lit up the whole top for an instant, and Zak saw that it was high enough that they might escape all but the largest flash flood. The mound of rock and dirt was at least two hundred yards long and half as wide. Nothing grew there, and the ground was soaked and muddy. But it would do, he thought.

He reined in Nox and turned the horse, waited for the others to surround him.

"Can you all hear me?" he asked.

They all nodded, their head movements aggressive enough so he could see that they had all assented.

"We're going to wait out the storm up here," he said. "We won't bunch up like you did back there. Instead, each person will have a station that covers most of the terrain up here. Kind of like a circle. It's going to be wet and windy. Probably all night. I'll check on each of you. You can hunker down under your horses, but look for anything that moves whenever there's light enough to see. And don't shoot me when I come riding or walking up on you. Any threat will probably come from down below."

Zak paused for several seconds.

"Any questions?"

"None, Colonel," O'Hara said.

"Call me Zak, or Cody, Ted. Drop the colonel from now on. I'm not in uniform."

"Right, sir," O'Hara said. "And I'd like to talk to you privately, Zak, when you're finished assigning us all posts."

"Yes."

Zak spoke to Rivers first, told him he would guard the rear of the hill. Both men dismounted.

"I shot two men when I culled Lieutenant O'Hara from that outlaw bunch," he told the soldier. "One was still alive when I went back for that horse. Never saw the other one."

"What happened to the one you did see?" Rivers asked.

"He won't mind the rain and the flood won't drown him," Zak said.

Rivers cleared his throat and saluted.

"None of that, either. Just forget I carry rank for now."

"Yes, sir," Rivers said. He held onto his reins and hunkered down underneath his horse's belly. He faced the back end of the hill.

"You'll face the wind, so get as close to the edge of this hill as you can," Zak said.

"Yes . . . um, yeah, Cody."

Zak smiled, but Rivers couldn't see it. He left the soldier there and walked back to the others. O'Hara was stripping the saddle and rifle scabbard from Cavins's horse. He handed the blanket to Colleen.

"Give you a dry place to sit for a while, sis," he said.

"Thanks, Ted. Where do you want me, Zak?"

"You can stay with your brother or walk ten paces along this side and take up that position."

"All right," she said. Zak thought she sounded disappointed. He brushed it off. He would talk to her later.

"Scofield, you take the point," Zak said. He pointed to the opposite end of the hill. "Keep a sharp eye."

"Yes, sir," Scofield said, and started walking his mount to the far end of the hill.

"I want you on this side, nearest the road, Ted," Zak said. "Close to Rivers, in case he runs into anything."

"You expect an attack from our rear?" O'Hara said.

"You never know."

"What about you, Zak?" Colleen asked. "Where will you be?"

"I'll be right across from you on that side, close to Scofield. You holler if you see anything that doesn't seem right. A stray horse, a cow, a man walking up the hill."

"I think I can handle it," she said.

"Ted, let's talk when you're finished and then you can go to your post."

"Won't take a minute." Ted finished attaching the scabbard to his horse and slid the rifle in its sheath.

"Colleen," Zak said, "you might go through those saddlebags your brother took off that horse and see if there's any grub there. Give the rifle cartridges to your brother."

"Glad to," she said cheerily, and Zak thought she needed a good slap, or a spanking.

He walked off toward the center of the hill and waited for O'Hara. Ted led his horse over a few minutes later.

"Go ahead, Ted," Zak said. "What have you got to say?"

"I just wanted to say that I don't think you need to press too much on following

Trask and Ferguson. I know where they're going."

"How do you know that?"

"Trask forced me to mark on my map where Cochise's camp was located. I marked them incorrectly. But I know where and how I marked them. I can find the spots easily, even without a map."

"That's good, Ted. Do you also know where Cochise is?"

"I know where he was, and I know the places he likes. For some reason, he trusted me."

"Cochise is a good judge of character."

"You know him, Zak?"

"We've met. Anything else?"

"Thanks for getting me away from that bunch. I have no doubt they would have killed me once they found what they were looking for."

"Or didn't find what they were looking for."

"Yes."

"All right. Take your post. I'll see you by and by."

O'Hara started to salute and caught himself in time. He grinned and walked off toward Rivers.

Zak saw Colleen sitting on the folded horse blanket under her horse's belly. He knew she was wet and cold. They all were. It could not be helped.

The wind was much stronger when he took up his position almost directly opposite where she sat like a drenched bird. He crabbed under Nox and patted the horse's chest, positioning him so his rear faced the wind from the northwest. It was all he could do on such a miserable night.

He worried about the lightning. They were all in the open and on high ground. A bolt could strike any one of them and fry their insides, boil their blood like pot coffee. And the snakes would join them. Might even see a deer or two, or a jackrabbit. It was a hellish place to be, and they would all be worn to a frazzle by morning.

He settled his rump on the cold, rocky ground and tested the looseness of his pistol in its holster. He might have to draw it fast, but wasn't expecting anyone to ride up on them during the storm. Deets might still be alive. That was the name Cavins had mentioned. Or someone else. But if he had any sense at all, he'd be on his own hill or somewhere out of the rain and wind, if there was such a place.

Trask was probably warm and dry in the nearest stage stop, the bastard.

Zak didn't want to think of him any more

that night, and he didn't.

Instead, he found himself thinking about Colleen, wishing he could hold her close and keep her warm. Lightning ripped through black clouds off to the south and west. The tremendous crash of thunder wiped out even those thoughts as he and Nox both shivered in the cold, relentless rain.

CHAPTER 10

The men in the adobe hut could all hear the water. They braced themselves in the darkness, pressing against mud-brick walls that might be washed away under tons of water at any moment. They forgot, in that moment, the stench that permeated the dwelling, the terrible odor of rotting human flesh, fecal matter, dried blood, the pungent scent of death that clung to the walls, ceiling, and floors like cave mold.

"Can we light a lamp, Ben?" Rawlins asked. "I can't see a damned thing."

"No," Trask barked. "Hell no. You just hang on, Rawlins."

The roar of water could be heard above the thunder. It sounded like something out of hell, a terrible liquid moan gushing out of the earth's bowels, louder than a locomotive's steam engine.

Trask stood near a window, looking out. Lightning splashed a brilliant glow over the land, and he saw a wall of mud and water speeding down the road. Behind the churning mass, he saw the flood tower higher still, as if some volcanic explosion were pushing it up until it swallowed everything on land in its massive voracious maw. Instinctively, he drew back from the window and threw his arms up in a defensive gesture.

Ferguson, a few feet away, saw Trask duck his head, and his eyes widened in horror and his gut knotted up in fear as a forked lightning bolt split open the darkness. A second later the adobe seemed to shudder from the thunder booming overhead. It sounded as if something had exploded inside the hut.

"What is it, Ben?" Ferguson said, his eardrums still reverberating from the sound of the thunder-clap.

"Brace yourselves, boys," Trask said. "There's a damned river out there on the road."

Ferguson heard the water. Fear clutched his throat with cold bony fingers. It sounded so close and so loud now.

The wall of water rushed past and a torrent struck the side of the adobe. Dirty water splashed through the windows. There was a loud screech as something scraped the side of the building, a board or a tree, something wooden, Trask thought.

Rawlins grunted. The Mexicans cried out the names of Jesus and Mary, in Spanish. Ferguson cursed. One of the Mexicans crossed himself. Those standing next to windows moved away from the wall and milled with the others in the center of the room.

A huge rock struck just below one window and knocked out three or four bricks. Water gushed through the hole and spread across the dirt floor. Trask jumped back and went to the opposite wall.

"Let's get the hell out of here," Rawlins shouted.

"We're all going to be drowned like rats," Ferguson yelled as more bricks fell away and more water rushed through the opening.

"You go outside, you're a dead man, Hiram," Trask yelled. "Everybody stay put."

"We are going to die," Hector Gonzalez whimpered.

"Shut up, Hector," his brother Fidel said.

The sound grew horrendous as the water crashed into the adobe, hurling rocks and debris against the outer walls. The flood ravished the side of the adobe, widening the hole, pouring more water inside in pumping gushers. Soon the entire floor was underwater. Rawlins saw a chair fall over and make a splash as still more water rushed in through the widening aperture.

"Ben, we got to get the hell out of here," Rawlins said.

"Damn you, Rawlins. Don't go loco on me. You go outside, that water will wash you away like a damned straw.

"What if that wall goes?" Ferguson asked.

"We'll get wet," Trask said. "We'll have three walls left and that's what will keep us from drowning, you dumb sonofabitch."

"Watch what you call me, Trask," Ferguson said.

"Then shut your damned mouth, Hiram."

Jaime Elizondo started muttering a prayer in Spanish. His voice quavered with fear.

All of the Mexicans moved to the opposite wall and braced themselves against it. Trask looked at them in disgust. Rawlins splashed over and stood with them. Ferguson hesitated a moment, then joined Rawlins. Trask stood alone in the center of the adobe, water up to his ankles and more pouring in through the hole. The bricks around the hole were crumbling, falling into the water, making plopping sounds. Outside, the flood raged on, growing wider and stronger, as if a dam had burst and released a deadly river.

"That wall's a-goin'," Ferguson shouted

above the tumult.

Trask could see it. The old adobe bricks were crumbling under the force and pressure of the water. The hole widened just above the base of the wall, allowing more water to eat at the bricks.

"Nothing we can do about it," Trask said.

"We have to get out of here," Fidel said.

"You go outside, you'll drown," Trask said. "That flood will pass. Don't nobody go off half-cocked here."

But he was worried that the flood waters would engulf them as more and more of the south wall began to erode and turn to mud. Some water was sloshing onto the east wall, too, but so far there had been no breech. The wall was holding.

He had seen flash floods before, but none as dangerous as this one. He had seen horses and men swept away in an instant when sudden water came out of nowhere and washed over a dry streambed. The impression was a lasting one, and he thought of one such flood now. This one was far worse, and all he could think of was that something must have held the water back long enough to build up to such proportions.

Part of the south wall was holding, but as the water ate its way to the door, the hole widened and they could all see the rushing water in the sporadic flashes of lightning. It was a truly terrifying sight, Trask thought, as water rose above his ankles and began filling his boots.

Some of the others were lifting one foot up out of the water, taking off their boots, shaking them out, then doing the same with the other foot. It was a losing proposition, and Trask just wriggled his toes inside his boots to keep his blood circulating through his cold feet.

"What about the horses?" Rawlins said. "They ain't hobbled. They're liable to run off and maybe get drownded."

"Better worry about yourself, Rawlins. Horses got more sense than you do."

Trask knew that panic was the immediate danger. He didn't have to look at the men to know that they were all scared, ready to bolt out into the storm rather than face death by drowning in an old adobe hut, trapped like rats in a rain barrel.

The best way to ride it out was to stay calm, he reasoned, and he knew that if he showed any sign of panic, some of the men would start crumbling just like those adobe bricks. He thought the horses would be all right. They were on higher ground. The flooding didn't seem to be hitting the entire east wall, but only sloshing against less than half of it on the south side. As long as that wall held, they should be all right.

There was a sudden tug at the building and a large chunk of the south wall shuddered. More bricks disintegrated, disappearing in a tidal wash of water. More water gushed in, and the level rose to Trask's knees. The thunder and lightning was still close and loud. The men jumped at every thunderclap, every stab of lightning. They had stopped emptying their boots, and through the murky darkness Trask saw them now looking upward, as if for a way to climb out of the adobe.

They weren't floating yet, but he knew they might have to start treading water if the flood rose up to their necks.

Ferguson swore under his breath, but Trask heard it. He turned toward the man and shot him a hard look. He could not see his face in the dark, but he hoped Ferguson would just shut up. It took only one voice to yell fire in a crowded room to stampede the whole bunch.

Elizondo began whining.

"*Callate,* Jaime," Hector Gonzalez said.

Then a broken timber slammed into the receding wall with great force, startling everyone. The log, or post, ripped a long gash into the bricks, crumbling them into granules that turned to mud as soon as they swirled into the water. More water gushed into the adobe, and the rest of the wall nearest the east wall began to break up, letting in gallons of water. It quickly rose above the knees of the men standing there.

Elizondo began to wail. It turned into a terrified scream, and he broke from the pack of men.

"Ya me voy," he yelled and started toward the door.

"Parate," Hector said. He stretched out a hand to try and stop Elizondo, but missed.

"Come back here," Trask said. "Jaime, don't open that door."

Elizondo, in a panic, continued to splash toward the door. When he reached down to open it, Trask drew his pistol.

Even in the dark, Trask could see Elizondo's hulk as he raised his arm, cocking his pistol. He took aim and squeezed the trigger. The loud explosion made the men jump. The flash exposed Elizondo's back for a brief moment as the bullet smacked into his spine, shattering the cord into bits.

Elizondo stiffened as his back arched in one final spasm. He let out a gasp and tumbled head first into the muddy water, paralyzed. There was a sucking sound as his mouth took in water. The smell of burnt powder and smoke hung in the air of the adobe.

The Gonzalez brothers gasped aloud. Another Mexican sobbed.

"Damn," muttered Ferguson under his breath.

"Bastard," Trask said. He did not holster his pistol, but turned to the men huddled against the wall.

"I'll put out the lamp of any man who tries what Jaime did. You all stay put, or I'll shoot every damned one of you before you take one step toward that door."

No one spoke.

Trask slid his pistol back in its holster. "Just try me," he said, glaring at the men.

"Nobody's goin' to try that, Ben," Ferguson said.

"They better not."

"Did you have to kill him?" Rawlins said.

"He would have drowned anyway," Trask said.

The water kept rising. It was up to their crotches now, and the men squirmed. They were wet and miserable. They could see the water with each flash of lightning, and most of them trembled in fear as water kept hurtling past the adobe. The thunder came from farther away now, but the rain and wind were relentless.

The water rose slightly, but now it was from the rain more than the flood.

Trask knew that if they could hold on for another hour or so, the water would go down and they could think about drying out, getting some grub in their bellies, checking on the horses.

His right hand never strayed far from the butt of his pistol.

The Mexicans would be angry, he knew, now that he had killed one of their number. They were Ferguson's men, but they were working for him. They wanted the Apache gold as much as he did, and that would serve to hold their tempers down, perhaps, keep them in check.

Ferguson would pay for his part in all of this, Trask thought. The men in the line shacks were probably all dead, killed by Zak Cody. So he could not count on them. He needed every man he had left. But he would not hesitate to kill any one of them who questioned his authority or tried to run off.

He would even kill Ferguson if he had to. The man was no longer needed.

The men who worked for the freighter might no longer be loyal to Ferguson, but they would be loyal to Trask. Or more exactly, they would be loyal to the gun he carried on his hip.

They would be loyal, all right, or they would die.

Just like Jaime Elizondo.

CHAPTER 11

Corporal Scofield yelled, "Something's comin'."

Zak heard it in between rumbles of thunder. He stood up and ran toward Scofield at the east end of the hill. The sound was unmistakable. He looked down but couldn't see anything because the sky was too dark.

"What is it?" Scofield asked.

"Flash flood," Zak said.

"Lordy. It sounds like all hell is breakin' loose."

"I think we're high enough so the water won't reach us, but stay on your toes."

Zak left Scofield standing next to his horse, shaking like a man in a quake. He ran to Colleen, who had crawled out from under her horse and was standing up, gripping her reins as if they were lifelines and she was on a sinking ship.

"Is that sound what I think it is?" she said to Zak.

"It should hit the road below us at any second."

Colleen cocked her head to listen. She could not exactly identify the sound, for it was like no other she had ever heard. It sounded, at first, like a giant's whisper, like air whooshing through a blacksmith's bellows. It did not sound like water. There was no watery sound. And then, as it got closer, it changed, and it sounded to her like a thousand distant hoofbeats, as if some stampeding herd of beasts were trampling the earth in a mad rush down the deserted road.

"It's such an odd sound, Zak. Isn't it?"

"You can't hear the water yet, but it's a flood. A flash flood. We're high enough here so that it shouldn't hit us."

The sound was louder now. Closer.

"You're very reassuring, Zak."

The rain blew against her back, rattling like dice in a cup as it struck her slicker. Not a soothing, steady sound, but ragged, uneven, reminding her at times of flung sand, at other times like buckets of water dumped from a great height.

He wanted to hold her close to him, protect her from the rain and the chilling wind. Instead, he put an arm around her shoulders to comfort her.

"You might get mud splashed on you, Colleen, that's all."

The two did not have to wait long. As more lightning laced the rain-heavy black clouds, they saw the huge wall of water roar down the road, its muddy waters raging, tumbling, churning, washing over the ground, eating up everything in its path.

She clung to Zak, leaning back against him, grabbing one hand in her own.

Colleen said something, but he couldn't hear her above the roar of the flood. He tightened his grip on her. It seemed that the hill trembled under the onslaught of tons of water, though he knew that was probably impossible. But he heard the terrible sound of the water as it splashed against the side of the hill, gouging out rocks and dirt, adding bulk to its dimensions.

Someone yelled, either O'Hara or Rivers, Zak thought, but he gazed down through the darkness and was mesmerized by the awesome power of the flood, the tremendous force it exerted on the road, the side of the hill, like some liquid dragon gobbling up everything in its ravishing path.

"Oh," Colleen cried out.

She was looking down, as he was, captivated by the sight of so much water traveling at such speed. The flood had a long downhill run, Zak knew, and would eventually fan out and subside. In the meantime, he wondered how so much water had built up and gathered so much strength. The rain was heavy, yes, but such a large flood was uncommon in desert country. He thought there must have been a lot of runoff to feed such a flood from higher ground.

There *was* a lot of rain. He had seen more, up in the Snake country, over in Oregon and Washington. But there were large rivers there, and here there were none. Once the ground was soaked full, the water had no place to go except overland, pushing through dry creek beds, over roads, and into gullies and washes, arroyos and gulches.

Colleen's horse spooked when it saw the water. It bolted away from the rim of the hill, and Zak reached for the reins. Colleen held on, but the reins were slipping from her grasp.

"Whoa, boy," Zak said, jerking down on the reins, digging the bit into the back of the horse's mouth. The horse fought him, bobbing its head up and down, twisting its neck. Zak bent the horse's head as he struggled with it, until its nose was almost between its front legs. He backed the horse away from Colleen and out of sight of the flood, then patted the animal's neck while still exerting pressure on the bit.

"You take it easy, boy," Zak said, his voice low and soothing. "Steady down."

The horse stopped fighting the bit, and Zak eased up. The animal shook its head, ran its tongue under the bit. The metal clacked against its teeth.

"He'll be all right now, I think," Zak said to Colleen, who had walked back over to him. "Just keep him away from where he was. Keep a firm grip on the reins, though."

"I will," she said. "Thanks, Zak. You sure know how to handle a horse. How are you with women?"

A bold statement, he thought. And from the way she was looking at him just then, he knew she expected a frank answer.

"Not much experience," he said. He was close enough to see her eyes, and his gaze did not waver.

"So you say. Not much difference between women and spirited horses. I mean their dispositions are similar."

"I wouldn't know, Colleen."

"With a horse," she said, "sometimes you have to be firm and sometimes you have to be gentle. It's the same with a woman, isn't it?"

"No argument there. But I wouldn't know."

"Wouldn't you?" That teasing tone in her voice again. Teasing, somewhat playful, he thought.

"Maybe a woman tells a man how she wants to be treated," Zak said.

"Oh, and do you always comply with a woman's wishes?"

"No."

"Zak, you don't mean that."

"A woman, same as a man, can be mighty unreasonable sometimes."

"So, if a woman's wish is unreasonable, you treat her differently?"

"I treat a woman the way she wants to be treated. I hope I do the same for a horse or a man."

"My, you are a mystery man, aren't you? A very mysterious man."

"No more than any other," he said.

She moved closer to him, until their faces were scant inches apart.

"I also think you are an experienced man. With women."

"What do you mean by 'experienced.' That word seems to be packed with dynamite when you say it."

She laughed, and the rain made her eyes sparkle as a ragged fence of lightning streaked across the sky.

"I think you know full well how to handle

women, Zak. And, I think you —"

"Don't accuse me of anything you can't prove, Colleen."

"Ah, you think I'm going to accuse you of something." It was a flat statement with a wicked curl to it. More teasing, he thought.

"I didn't say that. Look, Colleen, this talk doesn't seem to be going anywhere. We're in the middle of a big storm and there's a flash flood raging down on the road. This might not be the best place for a serious conversation."

She squeezed his hand with hers.

"You're the only real man I've spoken to in months. We schoolmarms have to take our conversations where we find them. I admire your honesty, if not your evasiveness."

"I wasn't being evasive. I truly have not had much experience with women. I've been a scout and a soldier for most of my grown life. Soldiering is about all I know. I don't go to any pie socials or afternoon teas."

"No, you don't. But I don't think you'd be out of place in a fine home with a bunch of flirting women surrounding you."

"I would be uncomfortable," he said.

She laughed again, and the sound of it was soft and pleasant to his ears. He was not uncomfortable with her, but was wary of falling completely under her spell. She was a very alluring woman, and for now, and probably for some time to come, he could not allow himself to be distracted by her charms.

The truth was, he had known a number of women, many of them almost as attractive as Colleen. Others were either too obvious, too shallow, or too brainless to attract his interest. The few good women he had known were either married or widowed, and the latter were often too eager to marry again and didn't much care who the husband might be.

"I think you could handle yourself, Zak. In almost any situation. And if you couldn't, you would say so, right out loud."

"I might," he said, and felt the powerful magnetism of her as she pressed against him, her face upturned to his, a wet face with moist eager lips and eyelashes that batted at the trickles of rain that seeped into them.

"What would you say if I told you right now, this very minute, Zak Cody, that I want you? I want you so much that I'm willing to forget my proper upbringing and fling myself shamelessly at your feet and let you take me, let you fulfill me as a woman, even though I'm a virgin and have fearlessly protected my virginity all my life. What would you say, Zak Cody? What would you do?"

He felt her arms grasp him around the waist, felt her pull herself into him, pressing so close that she aroused him. She rubbed against his manhood until it rose like an iron stalk between his legs and throbbed with engorged blood, surging against the bonds of his trousers like some ravenous beast desperate to penetrate cloth and canvas and break into her guarded portal and slake its lust on her willing body.

"I — I'd say," he croaked, "that the rain must have leaked into your skull and wet down your brain."

"No," she breathed, her breath hot against his lips, "I'm not mad or crazy. I'm burning inside with a womanly fire that I've never felt before. I want you so much I'm devoid of all shame and caution. I want you now, Zak, in the rain and the wet and wind, and I'd prostrate myself at your feet if only you would take me and quench these fires so deep inside me."

"Colleen —"

She flung her arms around his neck and pulled herself up, kissing him hard on the lips, taking his breath away. She burrowed into him with that kiss, and he felt the fire within her, the fire within himself. Her body ground against his and he wanted her then, wanted her as badly as she wanted him. He put his arms around her and held her tight against him. He pushed against her woman-hood, thought that he could feel its softness past all the material that stood between.

He closed his eyes and blotted out the storm. He no longer felt the needling rain, the bruising wind, or heard any thunder but the thunder pounding in his temples, his ears, and all through his body.

He felt her body soften and begin to fall away from him. He knew she was dragging him down to the soaked ground and the rocks, and on the edge of that cliff, he felt himself following her, stepping off into space, into a dark abyss where only lovers go, a place where all time stood still and nothing mattered but the moment, the desire, the fierce animal coupling natural to all sentient beings.

Then he heard a shot. He heard it through the thick fog in his brain, the cotton in his ears, the crush of her body on his senses.

"Halt, who goes there?" Scofield cried out, his voice carrying on the wind, like a warning klaxon.

It galvanized Zak out of Colleen's arms,

100

out of that seductive web of hers, and jolted him back to the precipice, into the world of the living, where danger rode the lightning, charging through his veins, electrifying his warrior self into being once again, where the only law was survival of the fittest.

The only thing that mattered.

CHAPTER 12

Scofield bellowed into the rain and the night, yelling at the top of his lungs.

"Halt, or I'll shoot."

Zak stood Colleen up straight. He squeezed her arms as if to make sure her feet were firmly planted.

"Stay here," he said to her. "Keep your horse between you and Scofield."

"Be careful," she warned as he drew his pistol and started running toward the sound of Corporal Scofield's voice.

Ted O'Hara was yanking his recently acquired rifle out of its scabbard.

"Back me up, O'Hara," Zak said as he jumped past the lieutenant. "Stay here."

O'Hara did not reply, but Zak heard the rifle click as Ted jacked a cartridge into the chamber. Scofield was standing up near his horse's rump, a pistol in his right hand.

"What have you got, Scofield?" Zak was breathing hard, but he wasn't entirely winded.

"Somebody's comin' up this side. I thought I saw a horse. He won't stop. And he's comin' mighty slow."

"Stand easy," Zak said. "I'll take a look."

"You watch it, Cody. Could be more than one."

Zak said nothing. He bent over and stalked to the edge of the hill, where he stopped, cupped his left ear and listened.

He heard what sounded like the snort of a horse. He thought he could see a dark shape near the base of the hill. The animal seemed to be well away from the raging flood waters, but unless it climbed the hill, a surge might wash it away.

A peal of thunder died away, and he heard a low moan. A man was on that horse, he thought. He held his pistol at the ready.

"H-Help me," someone said.

A man's voice. Very faint, barely audible against the constant tattoo of the rain, the blustering lash of the wind.

Zak eased down the slope, crouching, setting both feet before he took another step. He sidled toward the horse at an angle. He wanted to flank the animal and the man. He stepped like an Indian, careful not to make noise or to kick loose any dirt and rocks. Slow, short steps brought him around to the horse's left flank. He stopped to listen after every few steps.

The horse was pawing the ground, trying to get a foothold, Zak thought. The water had loosened some of the soil, and the horse didn't have sense enough to follow a switch-back course. And the man was obviously too hurt to take charge and guide the horse any farther.

Zak took a few more careful steps. He was close now.

He could hear the horse wheezing. He heard, also, the low groan of the man. As he stepped still closer, he saw that the man was slumped over the saddle, hatless, his arms hanging loose and straight down.

"Mister," Zak said, "you want help, you just stay where you are. You make a move, and I shoot you out of the saddle."

"God's sake, man. I'm hurt. Hurt bad."

"I have a gun on you. Just wait."

"Hurry," the man gasped.

Zak came up on the side of the horse, from behind. He stopped, reached over for the man's pistol. It was still in its holster. He slid it free, tucked it inside his belt. The man heard the rustle of Zak's slicker and looked over at him.

"Who —" the man said.

"Never mind. Stay on, and I'll lead your

horse up to the top of the hill."

"Oh God, it hurts."

"Where are you hit?" Zak asked.

"Don't know. I hurt all over. Belly, maybe."

"I'll take a look after we get up top."

Zak grabbed the reins with his left hand and pulled the horse on a straight line, parallel to the slope.

"You all right down there?"

Scofield's voice.

"Comin' up," Zak yelled back. "Wounded man."

"Come on," Scofield said.

When he reached the top, O'Hara was there with Scofield to meet him.

"What you got here, Zak?" Ted asked.

"Wounded man. Worn-out horse. Let's get him down and see what we can do for him."

"I recognize him," O'Hara said. "That's Al Deets. One of Trask's men."

Deets was moaning. He cried out when Scofield and O'Hara lifted him off the horse. By then, Colleen had rushed up.

"Take his horse, Colleen," Zak said. "Tie him to Scofield's over there."

She took the reins and led the horse away. In a few moments she was back, looking down at the wounded man. O'Hara and Cody were squatting next to him. Scofield stood watch, the rain battering him, the wind whipping his slicker so it flapped against his legs.

"Where's the most hurt, Deets?" Zak asked.

"Side. Belly."

"This man was shot," O'Hara said. "When you rescued me, right?"

"Probably," Zak said. "Hold his arms while I look for a bullet hole. This might hurt, Deets."

Zak unbuttoned the wounded man's slicker, then worked the buttons on his shirt, exposing his side and belly. It was dark and he couldn't see well, but he thought there was a stain across the man's abdomen. He rubbed there and then tasted the tip of his finger.

"Blood," he said.

Deets winced as Zak put his fingers to work, exploring the man's stomach and side. He felt something give. Deets jumped as if electrocuted when Zak probed the soft spot with his right index finger.

"Damn," Deets said. "That hurts like hell."

His voice was weak, barely audible against the relentless drumming of the rain, the angry whooshing sound of the flood along the road.

"Just lie still," Zak said as he continued to feel around the wound. He slipped his hand underneath Deets's back. The flesh was sticky with fresh blood, crusted with blood that had already dried. He finished his examination, tapped O'Hara on the arm and stood up.

He grabbed the crook of O'Hara's elbow and guided him away from Deets. He leaned close and whispered into the lieutenant's ear. "Come with me," he said.

Zak walked for several yards, then stopped and again put his face close to O'Hara's.

"Deets was lucky," he said. "He's not badly wounded. But I don't want him to know that."

"What?"

"He's got a flesh wound, O'Hara. My bullet plowed a hole in his left side. The bullet went clean through. He's lost some blood, but no broken bones, no lead in him."

"So, what do we do with him?"

"I want Deets to think he's going to die," Zak said.

"You what?"

"If he thinks he's going to die, we may be able to get some information from him."

"That sounds pretty close to torture, Zak."

"It's not torture. He's wounded. He has a bullet hole in the fatty part of his side. When

107

it gets light, I can find some clay to stuff inside it, plug up the hole."

"In the meantime, he suffers."

"He would have suffered anyway, if we hadn't found him. He might have bled to death if that wound tore up any more. We keep him quiet and talk to him. I think he can give us information about Trask that might help us."

"All right. I'll follow your lead, Zak. What do you want me to do?"

"Just back me up when I tell the man he doesn't have long to live."

"I can do that . . . I will do that."

"Good. Let's get started. He might pass out. I don't know how much blood he's lost, but he's weak. We have him where we want him."

The two walked back and squatted down on both sides of Deets.

"Deets," Zak said. "You awake?"

Deets moaned.

Zak bent over him. Deets's eyes were fluttering, but he was awake.

"Deets, I'll call you Al. You don't have much time left."

"Huh?"

"You've got a bullet in your gut, Al. You've lost a lot of blood. You're still bleeding."

"Damn."

"Maybe I can help you when it gets light. I might be able to get that bullet out and sew you up."

"You — You got any whiskey?"

"No. You'll have to bite on a stick."

"Shit."

"What can you tell me about Ben Trask? I want to know where he's going and what he's going to do."

"You go to hell. You the one who shot me?"

"I am. And I'm the one who can make your last minutes here on earth the worst you've ever had. I can make your last moments pure hell, Al. Is that what you want?"

"I ain't tellin' you nothin'."

"Suit yourself, Al. If I start going after that bullet, you're going to scream your head off, and if I find it, I'm going to push it in so deep, you're going to beg me to put a bullet in your brain."

"I — I don't want to die."

"Then tell me what I want to know. You've got two seconds to think it over, then I'm going to stick my finger into that bullet hole. If I can't go deep enough, I'll cut you with my knife."

"What do you want to know?"

"Tell me what Trask is after. Apache gold?"

"Th-That's part of it," Deets said.

A blast of wind washed over them, drenching them with gallons of rain. Deets squirmed in pain as Zak poked him in his side. He cried out in pain. His legs twitched in a sudden spasm.

"Just spell it out, Al, and maybe I can pull you out of this."

Deets hesitated. Zak pressed down on his wound with the heel of his hand.

Deets screamed in pain.

"Sorry," Zak said. He knew he was resorting to torture, but he wanted Trask so badly, he'd do this to get the information he wanted. In the name of expediency, he reasoned. If his shot had not been off, Deets might be dead now. A little pain wouldn't kill him. He felt O'Hara's disapproving gaze burning into him, but he didn't look at the lieutenant. Deets was close to opening up with the information he wanted.

"Don't — Don't do that no more," Deets said, his voice laced with the pain shooting through him.

"Then talk, Al."

"They — They's a group of citizens what wants the Apaches wiped out. H-Hiram Ferguson, he's behind it. But Ben Trask, he — he wants Cochise's gold. They mean to start a war with the Apaches. So's the army will wipe them out. 'Stir 'em up.' Th-That's what Ferguson said to do. And there's a big payday for all of us when the army goes on the warpath. That's what Ben Trask is after. The money and the Apache gold."

O'Hara let out a long breath.

"There's more to it than that, isn't there, Al?" Zak's voice was soft and steady, his tone coaxing, almost friendly.

"Wh-What do you mean?" Deets said.

"Fort Bowie," Zak said. "Someone there is helping Ferguson and Trask."

Deets sucked in a breath. The breath brought pain to him again. He threw an arm over his forehead and rode it out, gritting his teeth.

"Deets?" O'Hara said, eager to hear an answer to Zak's question.

Lightning scarred the skies a few miles to the east. Thunder rolled over them a few seconds later. The flood seemed to be losing force and there was only a faint whisper of rushing waters as Zak waited for Deets to tell him what he wanted to know.

The comparative silence seemed to last an eternity.

Scofield shifted the weight on his feet.

Colleen held her breath.

"You don't have long to live, Al," Zak said, his hand poised above the wound in Deets's side. "Time is running out. Right along with my patience."

Deets drew his arm away from his forehead and looked up into Zak's eyes. He could not see them, but he could imagine them. They were boring into him black as the twin muzzles of a double-barreled shotgun.

He could feel death coming on.

Death, he thought, was real close.

CHAPTER 13

Zak drew his pistol.

O'Hara reared back in surprise. Colleen let out an involuntary gasp.

Scofield drew in a sudden breath, held it.

Zak cocked the pistol, rammed the barrel straight into the open wound.

Deets stiffened, stifled a cry of pain.

"If you don't start talking, Al, I'm going to blow this hole so big you'll start screaming for me to put the next bullet in your miserable brain. It won't kill you right off, this bullet, but you'll stay alive long enough to pray for death a thousand times. You got that?"

"M-Major. It'sthemajor," Deets said, the words blurting out so quick they ran together.

"Willoughby?" O'Hara said in astonishment.

"Yeah — Major Willoughby." Deets started to shake as if he were passing apricot seeds. His teeth chattered, clacking together in a staccato tattoo.

Zak pulled the pistol away from the wound in Deets's side, and nudged the barrel against his temple.

"No lie, Al?" Zak said.

"No lie. Honest. Willoughby wants Cochise's scalp to hang on his belt. He — He owns land in town and round about. He wants every red Apache dead. That's what he told Ferguson and that's what he told Ben Trask."

"Shit," O'Hara said, and looked at Zak. "Can we believe him?" He asked.

"Ever hear of a deathbed confession, Lieutenant?" Zak said.

"No."

"Well, you just heard one. Deets was mighty close to death, and I think he just might want to live."

"Are you . . . goin' to fix me up?" Deets said.

Zak eased the hammer back down to half cock and holstered his pistol.

"Yeah, Al, we'll fix you up come morning. I may need you down the road."

"Need me? What for?"

"To testify against Major Willoughby when I bring the traitorous bastard up on charges."

O'Hara let out a long whistle. "Boy, you go right for the throat, don't you, Cody?"

Zak stood up. "He's your prisoner, O'Hara. You, your sister, and Corporal Scofield are going to testify, too. You were all witnesses to what this bastard told us. We've got a live snake in the woodpile at Fort Bowie."

"I can't believe it," O'Hara said. "Major Willoughby is a good soldier. Trusted."

"Those are sometimes the ones you've got to watch."

"Willoughby —"

"Don't worry too much about it. Just think about why he sent you out to track Cochise. Ask yourself that question, O'Hara."

"He — He said it was — was to protect the Chiricahua."

"You think Cochise needs army protection?"

"I don't know. I honestly don't know."

"Ask Cochise. If you ever see him again."

Zak walked away, leaving O'Hara to search for answers. Leaving him to think about his mission and why he was kidnapped by Trask's men.

Colleen came up to her brother, took him by the arm.

"You seem troubled, Ted. I hope Zak

didn't say anything to upset you."

"I am troubled."

"About Zak Cody?"

"No, he seems a straight shooter. It's just . . . well, he thinks we've got a traitor at the fort."

"Do you believe him?"

"I don't know what to think. But Zak may be right. Damn it, he goes right to the heart of a matter and lays it all out like it's gospel truth. I don't know what to make of it. I know General Crook thinks mighty highly of him. President Grant, too. But it's just hard to swallow that Major Willoughby would betray the army, would deliberately send me out so I could make it easy for him and Trask to wipe out the Chiricahua."

" 'Most everybody at the fort hates Apaches," Colleen said. "The only good one is a dead one, they say."

"Yes, I've heard that. More than once. But Cochise is following orders, same as me. He doesn't want to own land or build a settlement. He just wants to be left alone. To live his life the way he always has."

"You like Cochise?" she asked.

"I respect him. I admire him in many ways. He seems a man true to his own beliefs. I've smoked the pipe with him."

"But he's a savage, Ted."

116

"To the whites, maybe. But in his own world, he's . . . he's like a wise and kind king. I've seen him with kids, and seen the way kids and their mothers look at him. Oh, he's a fighter, all right. And I'd hate to face him in battle. But left alone, left to roam this desolate wild country, I don't think he'd be a threat to the white settlers anymore. He knows we're here, and he knows we're going to stay."

"I think you give Cochise too much credit. Too much honor, maybe."

"Well, I sure as hell wouldn't betray him. And that's what Willoughby seems to be doing."

"I — I admit I've grown somewhat fond of the Apache children myself," she said. "I taught them in another Indian village, you know. That's why I wanted to go to Fort Bowie. Their mothers are sweet, too, ignorant as they are about our ways."

"Dumb, you mean."

"No, not dumb. Ignorant. Not knowing. But even the mothers seem eager to learn new things. And they want the best for their children. They want their children to be happy and to learn."

"Maybe the answer is to bring teachers out here on the frontier, not soldiers."

"Ted," she said, "those are the wisest

words you've ever spoken."

"Colleen, get back to your post. It's still raining, and we can't solve the Apache problems between us."

"Yes, sir," she mocked. "And you're right. Who would listen to us anyway?"

"Not the army," he said.

The rain was beginning to slacken and the wind seemed to be backing off from its former fury. But there were still bolts of lightning ripping silver rivers in the clouds to the east and the rumble of thunder across the black heavens.

Deets groaned.

"You goin' to help me, soldier?" he said to Scofield.

"I don't know. Sir?" Scofield said to O'Hara.

"Corporal," O'Hara said, "you got a first-aid kit in your saddlebags?"

"Yes sir."

"Got any iodine?"

"I think so, sir."

"Pour some in this man's wound."

"Now, sir?"

"When the rain lets up."

"Yes, sir," Scofield said.

"Iodine?" Deets said. "That's what you got to give me? Ain't you got any whiskey?"

"Any more out of you, Deets," O'Hara said, "and I'll have Corporal Scofield pour the iodine down your throat."

"That other'n said he was going to sew me up. I hurt awful bad."

"I wouldn't count on Mr. Cody to make good on that promise, Deets."

"Mr. Cody? Zak Cody? Was that Zak Cody?"

"It was," O'Hara said.

"Lord God. That's the man Ben Trask wants to kill worse'n anything."

"I think the feeling's mutual," O'Hara said.

"Huh?" Deets was a voice in the rain and the dark. He lay flat on his back, spitting out rainwater.

O'Hara looked down at him without pity. The man had been his captor and was now begging for mercy. What's more, he didn't have the brains of a pissant.

"Deets," O'Hara said, "this is all going to seem like one of the best times of your life."

"I — I don't follow you, O'Hara."

"You're going to the gallows, Deets. You and Trask, the whole bunch of you."

Deets gasped, but said nothing.

"Keep an eye on him, Scofield. And don't be in any big hurry getting that iodine."

"Yes, sir," Scofield said.

O'Hara walked back to his post, his mind mired deep in a quicksand of thought. The ordinary world he had known, the army, had suddenly changed. First, he had been kidnapped, forced to draw maps and reveal secret information. Then he had learned that his own post commander, albeit on temporary duty, was essentially a traitor. Willoughby was defying military orders, contradicting the wishes of the U.S. government itself in order to further his own aims. He had brought his sister Colleen into this quagmire, this mess, and now it appeared she was about to give herself to a man with no future, Zak Cody.

He trudged to his former position, stood there as if alone on a small island. There was no one he could turn to anymore, no man he could trust, no one he could confide in or hold in confidence in the midst of his quandary.

Colleen was a grown woman, of course. But he was her older brother. He should be able to talk to her, to advise her, to warn her. But she seemed distant and alien to him now. He wondered if she had fallen for Willoughby at the fort. Was that possible? Had she even met the man? She didn't seem to understand the Apache situation. She might bear some compassion for the Chiricahuas, the children, at least, but not for Cochise and the others of his tribe.

And what of himself? Had he allowed himself to be deceived by an Apache with a price on his head? Once, he knew, the Mexicans had placed a bounty on Apache scalps. And now the Americans were trying to stir them up so they could be eliminated from the human race.

The storm seemed to embody the turmoil he felt. The lightning, the thunder, the wind, the rain, the flash flood, and now, in his heart, one flash flood after another, all roaring through him, drowning his emotions, smothering his ideals, strangling his honor, washing away his sense of duty.

He wanted to cry out, to scream, to run back to Deets and shoot bullets into him until his pistol was empty. But he knew that would not assuage the anguish he felt at Willoughby's betrayal, nor quell his anxiety over Colleen's attentions toward Cody.

And somewhere in there, in all that turmoil, was Ben Trask, a man Cody wanted to capture and bring to justice.

Cody. He was a mystery. He was a shadow rider. He came out of nowhere and he would ride on when his job at Fort Bowie was finished. He would not take Colleen with him. He would take nothing with him but his secrets and his shadow. Wherever Cody went, he left dead men in his wake, and maybe a few broken hearts.

That would be Colleen's fate, he was sure.

But what of his own?

What would become of him and his career in the United States Army? Would the stain of Willoughby be on his forehead, on his uniform, for all to see, for the rest of his days?

Ted raised his head and exposed his face to the falling rain. He should feel cleansed, he thought, but he felt dirty and ashamed, ashamed of his thoughts, ashamed of his commander, ashamed of his fellow humans.

And ultimately, he felt ashamed of himself, of his powerlessness.

There was a great force advancing toward him, and he felt defenseless. There were things, he realized, that could not be fought with sword or gun, but only with wits and courage.

Did he have such courage? he wondered.

And then he thought of Zak Cody. Colonel Zak Cody. General Crook trusted him. So did President U.S. Grant.

Could he trust him as well?

He lowered his head and listened to the patter of rain on his hat, the subsiding waters of the flood whispering below him in the darkness.

He wanted to sleep, to dream, to float away from a world that had suddenly turned into a hellish nightmare.

CHAPTER 14

The roof sagged where the adobe wall had once been, held up by the part of the wall that was still standing. Water covered the dirt floor, knee high. Rats swam up to the men who stood in the shack and tried to climb up their trousers. Furniture floated amid other rubble, rags, clothing, near empty air-tights, bottles, pots, pans, cups, and a myriad of unidentifiable objects.

Ben Trask stood two paces away from the gaping fissure and stared out at the receding flood waters. Ferguson, a half foot away, saw dead animals float by, even in the dark. The heads and tails bobbed up, tumbled, disappeared: prairie dogs, quail, a coyote, and a dozen or so dead rats.

"Gone down some," Ferguson said.

Trask lifted a foot out of the water, let the boot fall back with a splash.

"Yeah, only up to our ankles in here now."

"I can get my men to sweep the water out

of here. Maybe light a little fire to dry things out."

"No fire," Trask said, his voice like a steel trap snapping shut. "Have your boys sweep out that dead Mex. The water'll go away on its own."

"Christ, Ben. You don't have to be so all-fired hard. The man had a family. Worked five years for me."

"The man was a coward."

"Hell, we was all scared when that flood started rushin' in here."

"This whole deal's turning to shit, Hiram. You can't make it no better with your bawlin' over spilt milk."

"You could have let the man drown by his own self."

"Hell, that what you think?"

"Maybe."

"The whole bunch would have bolted for that door if I hadn't stopped your man."

"Maybe not."

"You're a poor judge of men, Hiram. I'm thinkin' we're not likely to find any alive at the other stage stops, damn it all."

"Aw, he couldn't have got all of 'em. That Cody feller, I mean."

"I know who the hell you mean, Hiram. And you're dead wrong. Cody probably rubbed out ever' damn one of your men. I just hope your man at Bowie comes through for us. We're goin' to be way short of guns if he don't.'"

"It's all set, I told you. Stop worryin', Ben."

"Just like these old stage stops were all set."

"I didn't know you had a killer doggin' your tracks, Ben."

"Well, if those other men of yours are dead, you're going to have to send one of the Mexes to the fort."

"I know. Willoughby's goin' to come through for us. He wants Cochise worse'n anybody."

"Has he got enough soldiers to do the job?"

"He says he does." Hiram paused, kicked away a rat that was trying to crawl up his leg. "I believe him."

Trask shook his head. He was weary and frustrated. Losing O'Hara had been a big setback. Now he had to rely on Ferguson and an army man he'd never met. So far, Willoughby had proven reliable. He had set up the kidnapping of O'Hara by Ferguson's men. But the entire operation hinged on Willoughby's support. Trask was a gambling man, but he wouldn't bet on this one. Not with Zak Cody dogging him at every turn.

"Hiram, maybe you'd better tell me the name of the soldier who's bringing the extra guns when we go after Cochise."

"You'll like this one, Ben. None other than the quartermaster at Bowie."

"Name?"

"He's a lieutenant, but he's plenty savvy. He's got holdings in Tucson, too, and big plans. His name is John Welch."

"And you trust this man?"

"I do. And so does Willoughby."

"Do you know how many men he'll bring?"

"No. Only Willoughby knows that. But I'm sure we'll have enough."

"Why are you sure?" Trask asked.

"Because Willoughby said there's hardly a man at the fort who doesn't want Cochise's scalp."

"I don't want any of them in the way when we get that Apache gold."

"Don't worry. The major says we can keep all we can find. He just wants to start a war with the Chiricahua while he's in command of Fort Bowie. Satisfied?"

"I reckon," Trask said.

The water inside the line shack was going down, ever so slowly. The wind was slackening, too, Trask noticed. The stench inside was still overpowering, and now there was the cloying aroma of polluted water, dead things, maybe mold. He wanted to leave, but knew it was too soon. There could be other flash floods, and for the moment they were all safe. He had kept Ferguson's men from going into a panic, and it only cost him one man — a cowardly man, he was sure.

Ferguson directed two of his men to carry out the dead body, put it in the flowing water. The two men bent to their task in silence and did not speak when they returned. But they both glared at Trask and he made note of the hostility. He not only expected their anger, he welcomed it, because he was a man used to treachery, on both sides of the coin, and such knowledge gave him the edge he wanted. Complacency was not a condition he tolerated, either in himself or in others. The complacent man stood to lose all he held dear, including, sometimes, his life.

Ferguson walked back over to Trask and stood next to him, gazing through the gaping hole that had once been an adobe wall.

"You waiting for that flood to stop running, Ben?"

"No. I don't care about that. It's still raining and at least we've got a roof over our heads."

"How long we goin' to stay in this cess-pool?"

Ferguson's questions were beginning to annoy Trask. The man was trying to get into his thoughts. To Trask, that was an invasion of his privacy. He didn't like questions. Especially questions that asked him what he was going to do when he was still figuring everything out.

"Hiram," Trask said, "ever notice how slow time crawls by when you're in a place you don't like much?"

"I never thought about it much," Ferguson said.

"Well, think about it. We ain't been in this 'dobe shack very long, but it seems like we been here for eleventeen hours, sure as shit. But we ain't. It's still rainin' like hell outside, water ever' damned where, wind blowin' a blue norther, and you want to go back out in it. Shit, you can't light a cigar or a cigarette, you're soakin' wet clean through your clothes, colder'n a well digger's ass, no shelter, no warm fire, nothing but mud and water and black night. Bite on a goddamned stick if you can't take it no more where you're at."

"Well, Christ, Ben, you don't need to go off on me like a double-barreled Greener. I was just wonderin'."

"Hiram, I declare. Sometimes you're a pain in the ass and the neck."

"Well, all right, Ben. Shit, I just asked a damn simple question."

That's what it was, Trask thought. A simple question formed in a simple mind. But he was getting cabin fever, too, and Ferguson had touched a bare nerve. He knew they would have to leave soon. As soon as the flooding stopped, maybe. That wasn't the most pressing thing on his mind, however.

Somewhere out there, on his back trail, Zak Cody was waiting out the storm, too. And he probably had O'Hara with him, maybe others. He knew that Cody was close. He could almost feel the man's eyes on him. The way he saw it, he had two choices. He could ride on for the rendezvous with the soldiers from the fort, hoping to outrun Cody. Or he could wait, maybe set up an ambush and kill Cody before continuing on. Neither plan offered much. A betting man would pass on both.

He listened to the pelting rain, the slush and slosh of the river running down the road. He thought he heard one of the horses whinny but couldn't be sure. He thought of wolves, but knew the horses would kick up a worse racket than a whinny if they were attacked. At least they were on high ground, well away from the flash flood. They would keep.

He looked around the room, unable to see much in the darkness. But he could make out the shapes of men against the wall, all huddled together like beggars. The water inside had dwindled to a muddy puddle, level to just above the soles of his boots, dank and stinking, muddy and choked with dead insects, rats, and other varmints.

Lou Grissom stood a foot away from the Mexicans. He looked composed. He never said much, Trask had noted, but he seemed capable. He had the look of a man who knew where he was and where he was going. Like his man, Willy Rawlins. He might be able to leave those two behind to take care of Cody, ambush him. But he wondered, would two men be enough? He did not know the Mexicans, but they also seemed a capable bunch. If he and Ferguson rode on, they could rendezvous with Welch and the soldiers under his command.

But could he spare Rawlins? And would Ferguson allow Grissom to stay behind? Might it not be better if they all stuck together and just watched their back trail, pushed the horses to lengthen the distance between him and Cody? To divide his forces now might put the entire expedition in peril.

"Hiram," Trask said, "I'm going to talk to you and the men about what we're facing after we leave here. Maybe we can figure out what our best chances are to meet up with Welch."

"You worried about that Cody feller?"

"He's out there. He'll be coming after me."

"Seems to me that's your problem, Ben."

"No, it's our problem, Hiram. Just let me have my say and we'll get the hell out of here as soon as we can."

"Just so I have a say in what we do, Ben."

"Sure, Hiram," Trask said, once again concealing his irritation with the man.

"Grissom, you and the boys come over here close," Ferguson said.

"Willy," Trask said, "come on over."

"What's in the hopper?" Rawlins said as he walked close to Trask.

Trask looked the men over before speaking.

"We got a situation here," he said. "Cody and O'Hara, maybe some others, are bound to be on our trail. I've already lost too many men, and Ferguson here has probably lost all of his boys who were holed up in these old stage stations. So, I've got to figure out what's the best thing to do. I'll give you all a vote. That all right with you?"

All of the men nodded.

"I can leave some of you here to bush-whack Cody and O'Hara. Cody's good, though. And fast. A dead shot. O'Hara, I don't know about. They may have help. Or, we can all leave this 'dobe together and ride like hell to meet up with the soldier boys who are going to help us. Now, question is, what do you boys want to do? Split up, some stayin' here to shoot it out with Cody and O'Hara, or all ride on? Think about it."

"I think we ought to stick together," Grissom said, much to Trask's surprise.

"Why?" Trask asked.

"Anybody knows you split your forces, you weaken the whole outfit. I was in the army once't and I learnt that."

"I agree with Lou," Rawlins said. "Together, we got a good chance if that Cody feller catches up with us and wants to sling lead. The more of us there is, the more chance we have of surrounding him and puttin' out his lights."

Juan Ramirez raised his hand. "May I speak?" he said.

"Sure," Ferguson said. "Go ahead, Juan. What's on your mind?"

"Together, we are strong," Ramirez said. "We are few, but maybe we are more than this Cody. I think we should ride together. We have lost friends already who were not with us on this ride. This is what I say and this is how we all feel."

Trask held up both hands.

"All right," he said. "You've convinced me. I think you're right. As soon as we can, we'll mount up and ride like hell. It's going to be rough, what with the mud and water and all, and we'll probably have to bat our way through this rain. But we'll stick together. As for Cody, and O'Hara, keep your eyes open and shoot them on sight."

All of the men nodded in assent.

"And one more thing . . ." Trask said.

He paused, and there was a silence in the room as everyone listened for his final words.

"Shoot to kill," Trask said.

CHAPTER 15

Deets screamed as the iodine burned through raw flesh.

Scofield clamped a hand over his prisoner's mouth.

"That ain't goin' to help none," Scofield said. "And, I got more to do. That was just to wash out the germs, feller."

"What else you goin' to do?" Deets gasped, the pain gripping him, surging through the nerve ends all around the wound.

"I got some salve here I'm goin' to pack in there, make that hole heal up faster."

"Take it easy, will you, soldier?"

"If I had a fire goin' I'd put a hot iron to it and close that hole for good. You'd likely jump about four feet off the ground."

Deets swore under his breath.

O'Hara appeared next to Scofield, pulling down on the front of his hat brim to shield his face from the rain.

"Corporal," he said, "if he yells out again, knock him cold with the butt of your sidearm."

"Yes, sir."

O'Hara walked back to his post, angry with himself for losing his temper. But Deets was one of those men who had been his captors. He was still angry about being kidnapped and held prisoner against his will. As a soldier, he was bound to avoid capture, and if captured, to use all means at his disposal to escape. He had not escaped, not on his own. Cody had been his rescuer, much to his embarrassment. He felt he had not conducted himself well, and so he knew he was packing around a lot of guilt. And that didn't feel good, he admitted to himself. As a career soldier, he felt this was a black mark on his record.

But his anger could grow legs and venture beyond himself to Major Erskine Willoughby, acting commandant of Fort Bowie. Willoughby was behind his capture, he was sure of that now. His scheme to wipe out the Chiricahuas was diabolical and traitorous. He had to be stopped. He had to be brought to justice before a military tribunal. But first, of course, there was the matter of Ben Trask and Hiram Ferguson. They were the enemy in the field. Willoughby was safe and out of reach at Fort Bowie. "Damn it all," he growled under his breath.

Scofield stuffed a salve into Deets's wound. Deets groaned but did not cry out.

"What's that you just did?" he asked, his voice quavering as he shivered with pain.

"Some kind of medicant we use to plug leaks in our boys. Keep you from bleedin'."

"It burns like fire."

"Fire would be better. If I had a hot coal, I'd stuff it down there. It would damn sure close off that hole."

"Damn," Deets said, and shivered again as if gripped by a cold chill.

Scofield stood up. "I ain't puttin' no bandage on you. Too wet out. You just lie still and let the medicine work."

"I ain't goin' nowhere."

"No, you sure as hell ain't. Next bullet you get will give you a permanent headache." He paused. "For about a half a second."

Deets shut up then, and Scofield walked over to his horse and returned the salve and iodine to his saddlebags. Then he stood guard over Deets, who turned his head to one side to try and keep the rain from drowning him.

Distant thunder rumbled, sounding like a game of nine pins in a great hall, and distant lightning made the black clouds glow with a pale orange light. The rainfall thinned to a steady patter, with only small gusts of wind to hurl patches of it to a misty spray.

Zak hunkered down under his horse's belly, squatting between his boots, Apache style, his butt just an inch or so off the wet ground. He thought of Deets and how lucky the man was to be alive. The night played tricks on a man's eyes. He knew that, but still, he should have shot more true. No matter. He had accomplished what he meant to do, getting O'Hara away from Trask and his men. Ted seemed a capable enough soldier. Someone had betrayed him, someone in the army, or he would not have been kidnapped.

So much rain in such a dry land, he thought. But he had seen odd weather before, in the Rockies and out on the Great Plains. The mountains made their own weather. One minute the sun could be shining bright, with nary a cloud in the sky, and the next, huge white thunderheads could boil up out of some hidden valley and bring rain or snow within the space of a pair of heartbeats. He had seen dust devils turn into violent twisters, and known winds that brought blizzards down from the north to a land basking in sunshine and warmth.

But he knew the storm was moving eastward, losing its strength. He could feel the air change, and the rhythm of the wind and the rain had shifted into a lower gear. The rain was no longer slanted, he noticed, but falling straight down, the wind gone, and there was less of it. He watched as the curtain of rain thinned and left spaces in the darkness. By sunup, he figured, it would all be over. Such fierce winds had driven the storm onward, and the clouds were losing their moisture so rapidly they would be puffs of white cotton before noon.

He heard a muffled shout and put a hand to his ear.

"Colonel, sump'n over here."

It was Rivers.

"Be right there," Zak shouted, and crawled out from under his horse, waddling like a crab until he could stand up.

His clothing clung to him and his boots creaked as he traversed the short distance to where Rivers stood guard.

The soldier was leaning over the edge of the hill. He stood up straight when Zak came up alongside of him.

"What you got, Rivers?" Zak asked.

"I dunno. I heard a rattle, like some loose rocks rollin' down there, and thought I saw somethin' big come up at the bottom of the bank. I thought maybe someone snuck up on us. I just caught a glimpse when some lightning sparked off in the distance."

"Is it still down there?"

"I reckon."

"Heard any more rocks tumbling?"

"No, sir. That's what's so spooky about it. I ain't heard nothin' since that kind of thud sound and them rocks clatterin'."

"You did right, calling me over, Private. Now, step back. I'll take a look. If there's another lightning strike, I might be able to see what it is."

"Yes, sir. I got the shivers from it."

Zak peered over the side. He saw nothing but darkness. The bottom of the hill was like a black pit. The water from the flood was still running, but not as fast, nor as noisily. He heard the water gurgling as it passed the base of the hill. He stared, without straining his eyes, moving them from side to side, trying to pick up some kind of shape out of the blackness.

"You go on over and stand guard by my horse, Rivers," Zak said. "I'll take this post until we find out what it was that made that noise. You did well."

"Thank you, sir. I hope it ain't no ambusher."

"Probably a dead animal."

"A big dead animal," Rivers said.

And then he was gone, sloshing through the rain to where Nox still stood, neck bowed, tail drooping and dripping water. Zak watched until the yellow slicker Rivers wore turned from bright yellow to the color of curdled milk. He noticed that Rivers didn't crawl under Nox but stood beside him, his head shielded from the wind behind Nox's neck.

Zak squatted, leaned over the edge of the hill, peering downward. He closed his eyes for a few seconds, then opened them again. He tried to distinguish what stood out from the blackness below, a shape, anything that was darker or larger than anything else. He fixed on a spot that looked promising and waited for the faint light from any distant flash of lightning. Several seconds passed and then he got what he was waiting for, a lightning strike some five or so miles away. The bolt threw just enough light for him to make out a shape sprawled at the base of the hill. He thought he saw a pair of legs rippling in a pile of water. Human legs, attached to a torso that left no more than a quick impression on his mind.

Something, or someone, was down there, but it was no animal. It was two-legged, most probably a man. He had seen just enough to make him curious. He judged the slope, figuring he might go down and be able to climb back up. He touched the butt of his pistol, eased it just a bit from its holster, then let it fall back of its own weight into the leather.

He stood up then, turned to where Rivers stood, some yards away.

"Private Rivers," he called, "come here. Bring my horse."

He heard a muffled, "Yes, sir," and the yellow raincoat moved. He saw the soldier lead Nox toward him, and he waited, holding out a hand to gauge the amount of rain falling at that moment.

Rivers came up, held out his hand with the reins.

"No, I just want that lariat," Zak said as he reached for the coiled lariat that hung from his saddle. "You hold Nox real still."

"What are you going to do, Colonel — I mean, Mr. Cody?"

"There is something down there. A man, I think. Hurt or dead, I don't know which. I'll use the rope to climb down and check what we have there."

"Yes, sir," Rivers said.

Zak uncoiled the rope, made two loops, one on each end. He settled one loop around the saddle horn and snugged it up tight. Then he threw the rope over the edge of the hill until it lay out straight.

He patted Nox on the neck. "You hold tight, boy," he said.

He stepped over the edge onto the slope. He grabbed the rope to brace himself, then started downward, digging in the heels of his boots at each step.

"Hold my horse fast, Rivers."

"Yes, sir. He's real steady so far."

Zak reached the bottom and held onto the loop as he felt around his feet with his hands. His fingers touched something soft. He squatted as he saw a man's face. No hat. He felt the man's neck, put two fingers on the carotid artery. No pulse. The man was dead.

There was enough slack in the rope for him to slip it under the man's body, up under his arms. He pulled the loop taut and then jerked on the rope.

"Rivers. Back Nox up. Real slow."

Rivers didn't answer. But the body started to move up the slope of the hill. Zak walked alongside, tugging on one arm, holding onto the rope with his other hand, both for balance and to help him with his climb.

A few moments later the body slid over the edge of the hill. Zak, out of breath, stepped up next to it and stood, breathing hard.

"You can bring my horse close now, Rivers," he said.

"Yes, sir."

Zak leaned down, slid the loop from the dead man's body and flung it aside. The man was on his back, his eyes closed. When Zak bent down to look at his face, he saw that it was a Mexican.

Rivers stood by, still holding Nox's reins. "You got you a Mex there, sir," he said.

"Let's see how he died."

"Maybe he drowned, sir."

"Now, who in hell would try to swim in a flash flood, Private?"

"I dunno, sir."

Zak grabbed the body by the shoulder and leg, tugged at it until the Mexican lay facedown. He ran his hands over the back of the dead man's shirt.

"Uh-oh," he said, and his hand stopped moving. He bent over and saw the bullet hole, right in the middle of the man's back. "Shot in the back."

"Sir, I didn't shoot nobody," Rivers said.

"No. Maybe Ben Trask shot this man. For some reason. Flood carried him down this far. Trask probably isn't far away. Maybe in one of those old stage stations."

Rivers said nothing.

Zak stood up. He didn't know what had happened, of course. But someone had shot the Mexican in the back. And he knew he hadn't done it. Even by accident. He could feel Ben Trask's hands all over this one. A man like Trask wouldn't hesitate to shoot a man in the back.

But why?

Maybe Trask had some mutinous Mexicans on his hands, he thought. Maybe Trask had blamed this man for the loss of O'Hara.

It didn't matter. Trask was losing men right and left.

If this kept up, the odds would rise in his own favor.

"What are you thinking, sir?" Rivers asked finally, after Zak had been silent for several minutes.

"I'm thinking this is one less man I have to kill to get at Ben Trask, Private."

"Yes, sir," Rivers said, and a cold shiver slithered up his spine like a wet lizard crawling up a tree.

The rain continued to spatter them as Zak slipped the rope off the saddle horn, untied the loop, and began to coil it back up, just to keep his hands busy. He wanted to grab Trask's neck and squeeze and squeeze until the man's face turned purple and he died

of manual strangulation.
The bastard.

CHAPTER 16

Gray-black crepe hung from the dark clouds like tattered shrouds masking the sun. The rain had stopped and the clouds overhead had turned to a puffy gray pudding over a storm-ravished land. The flood had passed on and disappeared into a porous earth, leaving behind its detritus, shreds of cactus and ocotillo, the carcasses of rats and snakes and other animals, rivulets of mud and streaks of washed sand and cobbled dirt. There was a slight breeze, a warm one, and Zak knew things would dry out pretty fast.

He saw no signs of life, nor any sign of Trask and his outlaw band. Nothing moved in the feeble light of morning. He walked to each post and told those standing guard that they could walk around and stretch their legs, shake out their soogans.

Colleen and her brother Ted talked together and munched on hardtack. Zak stopped a few feet away from them, doffed his hat to Colleen.

"We'll get moving pretty quick," he said to Ted. "I think Deets hasn't told us everything he knows."

"What makes you think that, Zak?"

"Doesn't make any difference. I'm going to see if he won't change his mind about his loyalty to Trask and tell me more. I have a hunch he knows plenty."

"You're not going to torture him, are you, Zak?" Colleen said.

"It's a nice morning, Miss Colleen. You ought to be dried out pretty soon."

With that, Zak walked away from them and headed toward the west end of the hill.

Colleen stared after him, her face a mask of consternation, her forehead creased, her eyes slitted. She quelled the impulse to throw a retort at Zak's back, and instead squeezed her raincoat by the collar until her fingers turned white.

Rivers and Scofield stood over Deets. They looked up when Zak walked up on them.

"Deets here don't seem so bad this mornin', Mr. Cody," Scofield said. "He ain't got no fever or nothin'."

Deets looked up at Cody, a questioning look in his eyes. His lips were parched, his skin pale. He was still soaking wet, but Zak saw that Scofield had put a fresh bandage over the wound.

"On your feet," Zak told Deets.

"I can't move," Deets said. "I got pain. No feelin' in my legs."

"Boys, get Mr. Deets here on his feet, and kick him in the ass if you have to."

Deets swore as the two men jerked him to his feet. He groaned and doubled over after his feet touched the ground.

"Deets, I want you to identify a dead man. You're going to walk to the other end of this hill or be dragged. Suit yourself."

"I don't think I can walk that far," Deets said.

"Deets, you got more than a scratch. You're lucky to be alive. But you got some more talking to do, and you can make it real hard or real easy."

"Maybe if I leaned on one of the soldier boys, I could might walk that far," Deets said.

Both Rivers and Scofield bristled at being called "soldier boys."

Zak looked at both troopers, his eyebrows arched.

"I guess we might could do that, Mr. Cody," Scofield said.

"Deets, you straighten up and try taking a couple of steps," Zak said. "Corporal Scofield will catch you if you start to fall."

Deets straightened up. He groaned in pain, sucked in a deep breath.

Zak and the two soldiers waited.

Deets put a boot out and took a short step. Then he put his weight on that foot and moved the other. He looked shaky, but no one lifted a hand to help him. He looked at Zak.

"Try a couple more steps," Zak said.

"Hell, he can walk good as you or me," Rivers said.

Deets gingerly put another foot out, then the other. He winced each time he moved, but Zak was satisfied that he could walk.

"Keep walking," Zak said. "Should tighten up that hole in you, make you heal faster."

"Like hell," Deets said.

"Do it," Zak told him.

Rivers and Scofield walked beside Deets. The three men followed Zak. As he passed Colleen and Ted, he motioned to O'Hara.

"Ted, you should come with us. I think we're going to find out a thing or two."

"Not from me, you ain't," Deets muttered.

Zak said nothing.

"I'm coming, too," Colleen said, falling in step beside her brother. Soon, all of them were standing over the body of the dead man.

The corpse lay on its back, black eyes dark as olive pits, staring vacantly at the mouse-gray sky. Deets stared at the face for a long time, his gaze taking in the deeply etched lines around the bared teeth, the lips pulled back in rigor, giving the dead man a ghastly frozen grin, the skin taut, dark as a tobacco juice stain.

"Christ," Deets uttered, a whispery breath behind the crisp sibilant.

"You know him?" Zak asked.

Deets choked out the name from a constricted throat as if the word had hissed out of a heavy clog of foreign matter.

"That's Jaime," Deets said, "Jaime Elizondo." There was a hoarseness in his voice that had not been there before.

"He one of Trask's men?" Zak asked.

"In a way, I reckon. He worked for Hiram. Hiram Ferguson. Jesus, what kilt him? Did he drown?"

"Lead poisoning," Zak said.

"You kill him, Cody?" Deets asked.

"He wasn't shot here, Deets. Flood washed him down here. I dragged him up. He was shot in the back, if that means anything to you."

"I don't know what you mean."

"None of us shot this man. He was killed by one of your pards. Maybe Ben Trask."

Deets swallowed hard. His lower lip began to quiver and his eyes turned rheumy. Zak could see that he was thinking about Trask, mulling over the possibility that his boss had shot Jaime Elizondo.

"Might be," Deets said.

"This could have been you, Deets," Zak said.

"Naw. Ben wouldn't . . ."

After a moment of silence, Zak broke in with telling words.

"You saying Trask wouldn't shoot you in the back if you crossed him?"

"I dunno."

"You know damned well he would, Deets."

"It ain't somethin' I think about a whole lot, Cody."

"Well, maybe you should. You know where Trask and Ferguson are going, don't you?"

"Generally. Maybe."

"He doesn't have enough men to take on the Chiricahuas."

Deets said nothing.

"He's going to need help. More guns than he has now. Isn't that right?"

"If you say so."

"The Apaches would wipe him out so quick he wouldn't have time to jerk his rifle out of its scabbard, Deets."

"I dunno."

"Yeah, Deets, you do. You'd better spill what you know about Trask's plans or you'll be the first one I turn over to Cochise for an Apache sundown."

"Wh-What's an Apache sundown?" Deets asked.

Zak uttered a dry laugh.

"It's not pretty. Something the Apaches do to a white man they don't like much. Something they'll do if I ask them to."

"I — I don't know much. Honest."

"Bullshit," O'Hara said. "He knows all about Trask's plans. I know. He's one of Trask's most trusted men."

Zak turned to O'Hara. "Maybe you heard something while you were a prisoner, Lieutenant. How much do you know about Trask's plans?"

"I know he's going after Cochise and his gold. That's about it. He thinks Cochise has a huge hoard of gold hidden somewhere on the desert."

Zak suppressed a smile. He knew better. But he wasn't about to say anything in front of the two soldiers and Deets.

"Nothing about meeting up with other outlaws?"

O'Hara shook his head. "No. I got the idea

153

he thought he had enough men. But I didn't know how many until we rode out of Ferguson's. I thought he was going to be badly outnumbered if he took on the Chiricahua."

Zak looked at Deets, who was moving both his lips to keep his emotions invisible.

"Well, Deets, are you going to tell me what Trask means to do, or do I have to beat it out you?"

Colleen gave out a low gasp.

Zak shot her a look that was meant to chastise her for daring to interfere. She lowered her head and put a hand to her mouth.

"I told you, Cody, I don't know nothin'," Deets said.

Zak stepped up close to Deets, looked him straight in the eye. Deets glared at him in defiance.

All the others held their breaths as the two men stared at each other.

"You ever have hard times when you were a little kid, Deets?" Zak asked.

"Yeah. Who didn't?"

"Lean times? When there wasn't much food to put on the table?"

"Yeah. What's the point, Cody?"

"Your mother ever say there was something at the door during those times?"

"Maybe. I don't remember."

"Think, Deets. She said you had to look out for such times, didn't she?"

"She might have. Like I said, I don't remember."

"Sure you do. She told you what was at the door, didn't she?"

"You mean, like when the wolf's at the door?" Deets was starting to squirm inside his skin.

"Yes, that's right. She told you to beware of those times when there was a wolf at your door. Probably you thought there was really a wolf at your door, didn't you?"

"I reckon. Well, us kids didn't really believe there was a real wolf at the door, but we knew what she meant. I still don't —"

Zak cut him off.

"Well, there's a wolf at your door now. That's me. I'm the wolf at your door, Deets. And, if you don't tell me what you know about Trask's plans, I'm going to open that door and start eating you alive."

"Shit," Deets said.

Zak pulled the bandage off Deets's side and pressed a finger against the wound.

Deets dropped to one knee. He groaned in pain.

Zak grabbed one arm and jerked him to his feet.

155

"The door's open, Deets. I'm coming in. I'm a hungry wolf."

Zak stretched out his hand, a single finger pointed at the wound in Deets's side.

"No, don't. I'll tell you what you want to know."

"Spit it out," Zak said.

"Well, I know some soldiers are going to meet up with Trask and Ferguson. In a couple of days from now, I reckon."

"Where?"

"Up at the last old stage stop on this road."

"Who's bringing the soldiers?"

"I don't know for sure. I don't think Ben knows, either."

"You ever hear the name Willoughby?"

"Yeah, I heard it. He's the soldier runnin' the fort — Fort Bowie. Ben mentioned him some. More than once."

"Is Willoughby bringing him the troops?"

"I — I know Willoughby is helping out, but just before we left Tucson, I heard Hiram — Ferguson, I mean — tell one of his men to skedaddle to Fort Bowie and see the quartermaster, tell him we were leaving."

"You hear a name?" Zak asked.

O'Hara cleared his throat.

Zak looked over at him.

"The quartermaster is John Welch," O'Hara said. "He came in with Willoughby and a bunch of other soldiers. I believe they served together."

"That's all I know," Deets said, staring down at the wet ground where his bandage lay, stained with the suppurated fluids from his wound.

"You've tortured that man enough, Zak," Colleen said.

"Miss Colleen," Zak said, "you don't know what torture is until you've seen an Apache sundown."

The words hung in the air like a warning.

Zak turned away from Deets, spoke to O'Hara.

"Saddle up," he said. "All of you. We can't let Trask meet up with those soldiers. We're outnumbered as it is."

"Zak," O'Hara said, "are you crazy? We don't stand a chance. I won't put my sister in danger, either."

Zak stopped and turned around to face him.

"Ted, I outrank you. I'm playing that card. You and the soldiers are now under my orders. We leave in five minutes." He turned to Scofield and Rivers. "You keep Deets braced between you. He makes one false move, you empty his saddle. Got that?"

"Yes, sir," Scofield said.

Rivers nodded.

"Now," Zak said, "let's burn what little daylight there is and light a shuck for that last stage stop."

Colleen glared at him, but Zak turned away.

He was a military man, but he knew he didn't stand much of a chance against Trask and Ferguson with the men he had under his command.

But that was a bridge he'd cross when he came to it.

And, he knew, he might have some help by the time they got to the last stage stop.

The old stage road led straight into Indian territory, home of the Chiricahua Apaches. And Cochise.

CHAPTER 17

Trask stood in a corner, his arms folded, his eyes closed. He had dozed like that for two hours or more. Ferguson had rescued a chair and was sitting in it, leaning against the north wall of the adobe. The Mexicans had taken turns sleeping in wet bunks. One of them, Fidel Gonzalez, stood guard at a window, his eyelids at half mast as he looked out over the crumbled wall. The land was a mystery of darkness, flooded over, earthy smells hanging in the air like a nightmarish odor borne of dead animals.

"You wake me when it's daylight, Fidel," Trask had told the sentry. "Or just before first light. Savvy?"

Fidel had not replied, but nodded that he understood.

Now he approached Trask and put a hand on his elbow. Trask jerked awake, startled, wide-eyed, caught for a moment in that

confusing state between sleep and wakeful-
ness.

"Yeah?"

"Es la madrugada," Fidel said. "The dawn.
It comes."

"All right," Trask said. He walked over and
put the toe of his boot in Ferguson's shin,
rousing him from his shallow reverie.

"Wh-Wha . . . ?" Ferguson said as his
chair rocked away from the wall and he had
to struggle to maintain his balance.

"Time to get crackin', Hiram," Trask said.
"See if our horses washed away during the
night."

The rest of the men came out of their col-
lective stupor, groaning, yawning, stretching, as if they had been roused from the
dead.

"Lou, you and the Gonzalez brothers go
check on the horses real quick," Ferguson
said as he rose to his feet, kicked the chair
away.

"Willy," Trask said to Rawlins, "you check
around outside."

"Yeah, boss," Rawlins said. He knew what
Trask meant. The man wanted to know if
Cody was anywhere to be seen. He hefted
his rifle and strode out of the adobe in the
wake of the Gonzalez brothers, mud sucking at his boots with every step. Lou Gris-

som got up off one of the bunks.

"I'll go with you, Willy," he said, grabbing his rifle and falling in behind Rawlins. "Anything to get out of this damned shithouse."

Trask walked to the opening in the wall, looked out at a bleak world overhung with gray, elephantine clouds. He adjusted his eyes to the faint light, stared at the washed-out roadway.

"At least the damned rain's stopped," Ferguson said, walking up beside him.

"It stopped an hour ago, Hiram," Trask said.

"Hell, I musta been asleep. I can still hear it, seems like."

"That's the roof leaking. Let's get the hell out of here. Lou was right. This is a shithouse."

"Men are pretty tired, Ben. Me, too."

Trask turned on Ferguson.

"You keep that to yourself, Hiram. I don't want to hear no whinin'. We lost time because of that storm. Time we got to make up, wearin' out horse-flesh. I don't want no slackers today."

"Hell, Ben, I was just —"

"I know what you were doin', Hiram. Best to keep your mouth shut about such around the men."

"I get you," Ferguson said, and started for the door.

Trask laughed and stepped over the broken wall and outside. Men were such damned sheep, he thought. If all the walls had been down and a door frame the only thing left standing, they would all walk through that empty doorway. Habit, stupidity, he didn't know which. He met a sheepish Ferguson and they walked up the rise, barely able to see the ground. The rains had washed the slope clean, pretty much, and dead vegetation was strewn everywhere. Little piles of rocks stood at the end of now barren rivulets where streams of water had rushed down to join the flood.

Trask heard the horses nickering up on the rise. Rawlins and Grissom stood a few yards up the slope, both looking to the west.

"See anything, Willy?"

"Nope," Rawlins said. "Can't see far, but it's mighty quiet."

"You keep an eye out until we all get mounted. I'll bring your horse down to you."

"Lou, you come on with me," Ferguson said. "See can we get some grain into our horses."

"Don't give 'em much," Trask said. "A handful, maybe."

"You got any heart at all, Ben?" Ferguson said as he puffed while climbing up the slope.

"I got the heart of a bull," Trask said, as if taking Ferguson seriously. "I just don't want them horses to founder. We got some ridin' to do."

"Welch will wait for us if we're not there on time." Ferguson was still short on breath, but he gamely trudged on up the slope.

"You know that for certain, Hiram?"

"We got maybe five or six days leeway. Hell, I just sent word to him yesterday. My rider probably won't reach the fort for a couple more days."

"You forget. I got Cody on my trail. Him and no tellin' how many others."

"I ain't forgettin'. You plan to outrun him? Maybe wear out our horses? We ain't got no spares."

"You can't outrun a man like Zak Cody, Hiram."

Ferguson was puffing so hard by then he could hardly muster enough breath to speak. He stopped and drew in breath through his nostrils. Trask didn't wait for him. He continued on toward the horses, counting heads as he walked.

Ferguson started walking again, but his lungs were burning.

"Too damned much gut," he said to himself, every breath a draught of fire.

"Don't give 'em too much fodder, boys," Trask said as he reached the men. "They'll have plenty of water to drink once we get goin'."

Ferguson caught up with Trask. He leaned over, hands just above his knees, struggling to quench the flames in his lungs. His belly sagged below him like an extra hundred-pound sack of oats. He wheezed like a blacksmith's bellows, and all the men looked at him with something like pity in their eyes.

"Jesus," Ferguson breathed, and stood up straight, hands on his hips.

"You better pray, Hiram," Trask said, a smear of sarcasm coating his tone. "That belly of yours is goin' to be the death of you."

"I know it," Ferguson said, still panting. "That old lady of mine feeds me too many frijole beans and beefsteak."

"It ain't the beans and beef, Hiram, it's the damn beer. You got to cut out all the B's in your grub."

The men all laughed, enjoying that moment of levity after a nightmare night and at the start of a grim gray day.

Trask looked back down at Rawlins,

beckoned to him. Rawlins turned and started up the slope, Grissom following a few steps behind.

"What plan you got for gettin' rid of Cody?" Ferguson asked as he walked to his horse and patted the animal on the neck.

"I'm chewin' on it," Trask said.

"Well, when you got it all chawed, you let me know, eh?"

"Which one of your men is the best shot with a rifle?" Trask pulled the makings out of his pocket, felt the sack to see if it was still dry. It was. He fished out a packet of papers, which was also dry, took one out and began rolling a cigarette.

Ferguson looked at his men. One of them widened his eyes. Ferguson nodded.

"Pablo Medina there. He's a right good sharpshooter. Seen him take down a antelope once't at better'n five hundred yards."

Trask looked at Medina. He was young, wiry, with high cheekbones, almond eyes black as tar, a stylus-thin moustache, square-cut sideburns. His cheeks bore the faint roses of Indian blood running in his veins.

"Medina, huh? He don't look like much," Trask said. "Could have been a lucky shot."

"He takes down deer, runnin' deer, all the time at better'n two hunnert yards, Ben. The man's got a feel for a rifle, any rifle.

165

But that's a new Winchester in his boot. He bore-sighted hisself and he shoots one- and two-inch groups on targets real regular. Sometimes, I think Pablo cut his teeth on a rifle barrel. Comes real natural to him."

"All right. I'll take your word for it," Trask said.

"Want me to call him over?"

"Not yet. What about Grissom? Can he shoot?"

"He's a fair shot, all right. But Pablo, he's the best I ever seed."

Rawlins and Grissom came up.

"Didn't see nothin', Ben," Rawlins said. "Lou didn't see ner hear nothin', either."

"All right, Willy. See to your horses, you and Lou."

In the gauzy light of a gray morning, a lone hawk soared overhead. A sign of life after a deluge, Trask thought. He watched the hawk float over a desolate land, some parts of it still invisible, for the sun had not yet risen. He heard the far-off yelp of a coyote, and the horses twisted stiffened ears to locate the sound, their rubbery nostrils sniffing the still, cool air.

Trask turned to Ferguson, who was just reaching for his saddle horn to pull himself aboard his horse.

"How far you reckon to the next old sta-

166

tion, Hiram?"

"A long day's ride, Ben. On muddy ground, maybe longer."

"Cody will surely follow the road, same as us. If that 'dobe is still standing, maybe I'll leave that Mex sure-shot there to bushwhack Cody."

Ferguson pulled his arm down, turned toward Trask.

"You might be committing Pablo to a death sentence. Cody's got O'Hara with him. That's two against one right there. And you think this Cody ain't by hisself. Might be Pablo would have to go up against a dozen or so rifles."

"Might be. But he drops Cody, he's got a good chance to make his getaway. If he can shoot and kill as far away as you say, he'd have a good chance to outrun O'Hara or them others. A man drops in a bunch, the rest all gawk and hightail it for cover until they figure out what the hell happened."

"That's so," Ferguson said. He scratched the back of his head, tipping his hat forward. "I don't know. I'd hate to lose Medina. He's a good man. Got him a family, two little kids."

"All the more reason he'd watch after his own hide after he kills Cody."

"You make it sound real easy, Ben."

They were whispering, almost, speaking in low tones, but the other men were looking at them. They were all on horseback, just waiting for Ben's or Hiram's orders. The horses switched their tails and tamped the ground with their forefeet, pawing dirt with their hooves.

"I'll talk to Pablo on the ride to the next station, Hiram. Feel him out, see what he thinks about the whole idea. That good enough? If he don't want to do me this favor, no hard feelings. I'll get Willy to stake out that 'dobe and put some lead in Cody. Fair enough?"

"Fair enough, I reckon. Seems to me, though, that you put a lot of your chips down on rubbing out one man. He must have really got under your hide, Ben."

"It goes back a long way," Trask said.

He walked to his horse and hauled himself into the saddle. Ferguson mounted his horse. All of the men were still wearing their slickers. Trask made a face and took off his raincoat.

"Pack them slickers away," he said to the others. "You look like a bunch of yaller flowers. Anybody trailin' us could spot you ten miles away."

The men all removed their soogans and tied them to the backs of their saddles.

"Lead the way, Hiram," Trask said. "I'll ride with Medina. Gus and Willy can take up the rear. We'll go two by two. Pick your man to side you."

Ferguson motioned to Fidel Gonzalez, who rode up alongside him. Trask beckoned to Medina.

"You ride with me, Pablo," he said. "We got some fat to chew."

"Huh?" Medina said.

"Want to talk to you. Some palaver."

"Yes. We ride together. You talk. I listen."

Trask smiled. This was going to be easier than he thought. Medina might be just the man to get Cody off his back forever.

A thin line of pale light appeared on the eastern horizon. The sun was just edging up out of the darkness, casting an eerie glow over the land, tingeing the far clouds with cream and the faintest glimmer of gold.

Ferguson set a good pace, one that the horses might keep up for a good long stretch, Trask thought.

Trask smiled and looked over at Medina.

"So," he said, "ever kill a man, Pablo?"

CHAPTER 18

Al Deets was going to be a problem. He already was, Zak thought. The man was doubled over, puking onto the ground, while Rivers and Scofield stood on either side of him, averting their eyes so they didn't have to look at the vomit. They could avoid looking at the puke, but they couldn't escape its smell. Deets's face was florid, then drained of color as he finished retching. He stood up and sucked air into his lungs.

Colleen watched all this with a mingled look of compassion and disdain on her face. Zak shifted his gaze to her. She must have caught the movement of his head because she turned and looked at him from a few yards away. Her brother Ted was checking the cinches on her saddle, making sure they were snug but not too tight.

"You all finished throwing up, Deets?" Zak asked.

"I reckon." Deets wiped a sleeve across his mouth.

"Should I put another bandage on that wound, Mr. Cody?" Scofield asked.

"No, he'll be fine," Zak said. He held out his black slicker to Scofield. "Put this on him, Corporal."

"You want him to wear your slicker, Mr. Cody?"

"That's what I said."

Scofield took the slicker and helped Deets put his arms through the sleeves.

"Button it up good," Zak said, taking off his hat. He removed the hat from Deets's head and put it on his own. They were about the same size. Then he put his hat on Deets's head, squared it up, made it fit tight.

"What's all that for?" Colleen asked.

"We want him to look nice, don't we?"

Then Zak turned to the two soldiers.

"Put him up on my horse," he said. He walked to his horse and pulled his rifle out of its scabbard. The two soldiers stood there, looking puzzled.

"You want him to ride that fine black horse of yours?" Scofield said.

"And I'll ride his."

Deets looked pale, bewildered. The soldiers still stood there, as if uncertain that they had heard right. Rivers looked at Scofield, then back at Zak. Deets made some ugly sounds in his throat. Scofield stepped away from him. So did Rivers. But Deets didn't throw up again. He swallowed and his eyes watered, but he stood there, looking forlorn and lost in that black slicker and under Zak's black hat.

"Get Deets up on that horse, now," Zak told Scofield. "Then tie his hands. Loop the rope through that hole between the horn and the seat."

"Yes, sir," Scofield said. "Soon as he gets through bein' sick."

"He's through," Zak said. He stood, holding Nox's reins, avoiding Colleen's penetrating gaze. He looked to the eastern sky, saw the horizon brim with a pale light, a light tangled up in blankets of gray clouds. Some of the clouds began to brighten, with thin rims of gold that flickered and paled to yellow rust as they drifted toward the horizon, swallowing up some of the scraps of that feeble light.

"Zak," Colleen said, striding toward him, "I want to talk to you."

"Not now," he said.

"Now, Zak."

He saw that she was determined, and she looked as if she had something in her craw, all right. He shrugged.

"Make it quick."

"Privately," she said, taking his arm and leading him away from the others.

"You got some push in you," he said. "I'll give you that."

"Maybe it's time somebody did push you, Zak Cody."

"Uh-oh. When you use both my names, I know you're mad."

"Damned right I'm mad."

He could see the flare of anger in her blue eyes. There was an ocean in her, and he knew he was seeing only a small part of its surface. He felt drawn to her by those sparkling eyes, mesmerized by the clarity he saw in them. She was like a striking serpent at that moment, and he felt impaled on an invisible thorn.

When the two were well out of earshot of the others, Colleen released her grip on his arm.

Again she skewered him with her piercing gaze.

"What's the matter with you?" he asked.

"With me? Zak Cody, I didn't take you for a cruel man. Not once, since I met you. But the way you treat that man — that Deets — is just deplorable. Now you are going to have him tied to his horse like a — a trophy — or something you've shot."

"I did shoot him. But that's not why I'm having him tied to his horse. Deets is a dangerous man."

"And you tortured him. You know the man is wounded, so you deliberately touched his wound to make him talk. That's torture."

"Ma'am, I think you missed your calling."

"My calling?"

"Yes, you ought to be a missionary, going out and saving the miscreants of this world from the likes of me."

"Don't try to make light of this, Zak Cody. You're a cruel man, after all."

"That man, Deets, had important information. Vital information. His boss, a man named Ben Trask, is joining up with a military detachment to stir up a war with the Chiricahua Apaches. Now that's cruel, little lady. Not what I did to Deets. I just touched him on a sore spot."

"Don't you call me 'little lady,' you — you scalawag. Oh, what an arrogant, self-righteous man you are. I could . . ."

"Could what?"

"I . . . I don't know. Scratch your eyes out, maybe."

Zak laughed, but it was a mirthless and wry laugh that was not without a touch of scorn.

"Now, scratching a man's eyes out," he said, "that would be cruelty. To a high degree."

"You know what I mean," she said, miffed by his logic.

"This is war, Colleen. I needed information from Deets. I got it. You could call it torture if I got the information and then kept hurting him. I gave him a nudge. He told me what I needed to know. Don't try and make something out of it that it isn't."

"I guess I just don't understand you, Zak," she said, her manner softening.

"That's another matter entirely. Something you'll have to work out for yourself."

"Oh, you are an exasperating man."

"That, too," he said, a flicker of a smile on his face.

In the distance he heard a coyote yelp. The sound only emphasized how quiet it was after the rain and the flood. In the east, he saw a glimmer of pale light, a faint trace of salmon on some of the clouds, a shimmering tinge of gold that quickly disappeared.

"I wish I knew you better," she said.

"Who can really know someone, Colleen? People are mysteries."

"Mysteries? I've never heard that before."

"You can never truly know a person, Colleen. People wear masks. People hide who they really are. If you observed a single person all your life, every day and night, you still would only see a little bit of that person."

"I've never thought of people that way," she said.

"I have."

He started walking away from her. She opened her mouth to stop him, to pursue the conversation, perhaps, but instead just shook her head and followed him.

When Zak got back to his horse, he took Deets's rifle out of the scabbard on his saddle and replaced it with his rifle. He tied Deets's rifle in back of his cantle, after wrapping it in his bedroll and retying the bundle.

"Zak, got a minute?" O'Hara said to him.

"Less than that, Ted. We need to get moving. Trask is probably gaining more ground on us."

"It's about Deets." O'Hara's voice was pitched low so the others, including their prisoner, wouldn't overhear him.

"What about Deets?" Zak asked.

"Why are you trading horses with him and why did you dress him in your slicker and hat?"

"If Trask means to pick me off when we

get close, he might mistake Deets for me."

"I don't think Deets will make it very far."

"You mean Trask will shoot him instead of me?"

"He'll probably bleed to death."

"He might."

"I say we ought to leave him here. He might stand a chance, if we leave him some food and water."

"Your kindness is admirable, Ted."

"I'm not trying to be kind. Colleen and I think that man's been tortured enough. Now you want to make him a target for Trask. That's pretty damned cruel."

"It's not meant to be. Deets has a better chance of surviving his wound if he comes with us. Scofield can doctor him. As for Deets being a target instead of me, I call that simple justice."

"Not in my book."

"Maybe you ought to get another book, Ted."

"Look, I know you're a hard man, but Colleen is pretty upset. And I think she's right."

"Well, if Colleen's right and you're backing her, maybe you and she ought to go on to Tucson or make it to Fort Bowie on your own."

"If I left with Colleen, I'd take Scofield

and Rivers with me."

Zak shrugged. He saw that the day was getting lighter by the moment. They had already spent too much time getting ready to pick up Trask's trail. And the outlaw would leave tracks. Tracks that had to be followed.

"Ted, that's fine with me. You can all go to Fort Bowie. I won't try and stop you."

"We'd take Deets with us."

Zak felt his anger begin to boil. He knew he could pull rank on O'Hara and order him to stay. But he didn't want to do that. What galled him was that Ted and his sister were trying to protect a man who deserved no consideration whatsoever. Deets was a killer. He was the enemy. And he was something else.

"Deets is my prisoner, Lieutenant O'Hara. You can leave if you like, but Deets stays."

"So he can be killed."

"So he can be employed in a military situation, if you want it that way."

"Splitting hairs, Cody."

"My hairs to split. Now make up your mind. You can go with me to try and stop Trask and Ferguson from meeting up with renegade soldiers, or you can tuck your tail between your legs and crawl back to the fort. I'm sure Willoughby will welcome you with open arms."

"You do make a point there, Zak."

"Well, which is it, Ted?"

"I'm concerned about my sister."

"Maybe you'd better take her to some safe place. Tucson, Fort Bowie."

O'Hara sighed. "Knowing her," he said, "she wouldn't go."

"I can't guarantee her safety, or anyone else's for that matter. I'm after a bunch of killers and they want to start a war. That's a lot of lives at stake, Ted. I'm all out of argue with you, so I'm going to do what I have to do. You follow your own path."

With that, Zak climbed up into the saddle. He and Deets were the only ones who were mounted. Scofield and Rivers stood on either side of Nox, holding the horse still. Scofield held onto the reins.

"Come on, Deets," Zak said, riding up to him. "Follow me."

"What about us?" Scofield asked.

Zak leaned down and snatched the reins out of his hand.

"I'm turning you over to the lieutenant. He'll give you your orders from now on."

Zak rode off then, leading Deets.

There was a silence in his wake, and then he heard Colleen's voice.

"Ted, what is going on?" she asked her

brother.

"Damn that man," Ted said.

Zak smiled to himself as he rode down off the hill, Deets behind him.

There was more talk, more arguing, but Zak couldn't hear the words. Five minutes later he heard the clatter of small stones. He looked back to see Ted, Colleen, Rivers, and Scofield riding down the slope in single file. He wondered if they would cut across the road and head for Fort Bowie or turn down it and head west to Tucson. He kept going.

"Hold up, Zak," O'Hara called out. "We're going with you."

"Catch up, then, Ted. I'm going on."

He heard hoofbeats as O'Hara put his horse into a gallop. A moment later he was riding alongside.

"Zak, you're hard to deal with," O'Hara said.

Zak said nothing.

"Colleen said we ought to go with you. So, I'm putting myself under your command."

"Make sure Rivers and Scofield know that, Ted. And have them ride up here and take Deets in tow. I'm going to scout ahead. Stay alert. All of you."

"Yes, sir," O'Hara said, and turned his

horse to ride back to the others and issue orders.

The day brightened, illuminating the landscape ahead. He would stay off the road for a time. He knew they were not far from one of the old stage stops. There, he might learn something. For now, his gaze roved the land, looking for any movement, anything out of the ordinary. Sprays of lemony light shot through distant clouds on the horizon. He watched a hawk float overhead, wings outstretched, head turning from side to side as it hunted.

The stillness of morning made him feel good inside.

He looked back at Deets.

Deets glowered at him, and Zak nodded. The man still had some fight in him. That would help him if he was going to pull through.

The wound wouldn't kill him.

But Trask might, he thought.

Over that possibility, Zak knew he had no control.

But Fate might.

CHAPTER 19

Trask rode alongside Pablo Medina for two or three miles before he started asking him questions. He was sizing the man up, watching the way he rode, how he looked over the country. He wanted to see if Pablo had any horse sense. He also wanted to know if he was too inquisitive. He would have expected Pablo to start asking questions, but he did not; he kept his silence. To Trask, that was a point in his favor.

Pablo seemed alert. His head turned from side to side as they rode, and Trask saw that he was looking all around, his hand not far from the butt of his pistol or, for that matter, the stock of his rifle in its boot. He seemed at home in the saddle. He rode easy, but his left hand kept a firm grip on the reins.

"You got a family, Pablo?" Trask looked over at him to gauge his reaction to the question.

"I have a wife and a baby son," he said, his English only faintly accented.

"You born in Mexico?"

"Santa Fe."

"School?"

"Yes. I went to school."

"You didn't answer my first question. I asked you if you'd ever killed a man."

"I heard you ask, Mr. Trask," Pablo said, a note of respect in his voice. "I do not know how to say it."

"Yes or no. Simple."

"Not so simple. But, yes. I have killed a man before. More than one. I think you ask if I have shot a man with a rifle. I have not."

"Who did you kill?"

"My brother. And, my father."

"That's pretty close to home."

"My brother raped my wife. I caught him in the bed with her."

"And your father?"

"I see him in bed with my sister. She was screaming."

"How did you kill them?"

"I use the knife."

"You live with it. Aren't you afraid you will go to hell for killing your father and your brother?"

"If I do, I will meet them there."

Trask thought about what Pablo had said.

It told him very little about the man. Medina was either simple-minded or wasn't bothered much by killing another human being. He hoped Pablo felt the same way he did about killing a man. When you took a man's life, you robbed him of everything, of all power, and thereafter, that man's power was yours to use for your benefit. That was the kind of man Trask admired and respected. No quarter, no live and let live, but rather, live and don't let live, anybody who stood in your way.

Now that the sun was up, the clouds took on a blue cast, a pale lavender to their underbellies. And here and there, to the south and north, he saw streaks of white where the clouds were shredding up, dissipating and showing patches of faint blue that might have been sky, but he wasn't sure.

"Tell me, Pablo," he said, "how do you feel about killing a man you don't even know, a man who did you no harm, who didn't rape your sister or bed your wife?"

"I do not think of such things, Mr. Trask."

"Maybe you oughta."

"What?"

"If I asked you to kill a man, shoot him off his horse from some distance, could you do that?"

Pablo thought about that for a moment or two.

"Mr. Ferguson, he say I might have to kill somebody if I come to work for him. I say, okay. You pay me, I kill anybody. I tell him — Mr. Ferguson — you pay me to shoot you and I shoot you. He laugh and I laugh. It is a joke."

"A joke, yeah. But did you mean what you said? That you would kill anybody if he, or someone like me, asked you to do it?"

"When I was a boy, I worked on a big ranch. The boss told me when I work there, I ride for the brand. He mean —"

"I know what he meant, Pablo."

"I ride for the brand," Pablo said. "Always."

"That's good enough for me," Trask said.

"You want me to kill somebody, Mr. Trask?"

"That man who took the soldier away from us. I want you to kill him."

"Where is this man?"

"I think — I know — he's on our trail. I want you to hide out at the next stage stop and shoot him when you see him. He will probably be with the lieutenant — O'Hara — maybe some others. But you will shoot him first when you see him. He's easy to spot. He wears black clothes and he rides a

185

black horse."

"This is the man you want me to kill?"

"On the first shot, Pablo."

"He is the one they call *jinete de sombra,* no?"

"What does that mean? I don't speak the Spanish."

"The rider of shadow."

"Shadow Rider. Yeah, they call him that. He's the one. The bastard."

"Un carbon," Pablo said. "That is what they say he is."

"Could you kill him?"

"If I see him, I could kill him. Yes."

"That's what I want you to do, Pablo. There's a hundred dollars for you if you do that for me."

"I will do it."

"And, if you also kill O'Hara, the army lieutenant, I will give you another fifty dollars."

"Silver or gold?"

Trask laughed. "Gold, if you want it."

"I like the gold," Medina said.

"When the time comes, I will tell you what to do, Pablo. Think about it. Think about that shot."

"When will I do this?" Pablo asked.

"Maybe tomorrow. I'll let you know."

"Good," Pablo said, and Trask touched a

finger to his hat in salute and rode off to join Ferguson at the head of the column.

The blue in the sky softened and the white streaks grew larger and longer, the wind sculpting the clouds. The lavender was fading, giving way to patches of the purest blue, as if a giant ceramic bowl had been glazed in a kiln and was just emerging into the cool high reaches of the atmosphere. Trask studied the sky and thought it was going to be a good day when the sun broke through and dried the road where travel would be easier.

"You and Pablo come to an agreement?" Ferguson asked when Trask rode up alongside him.

"I think so. We'll leave him at the next stage stop while we ride on."

"You payin' him?"

"I said I would. Why?"

"Just curious. I hope it works out. This Cody feller, from all I've heard, is a pretty tough bird."

"No man can stop a bullet, Hiram."

"I just hope Pablo doesn't stop one."

The ground they traveled was witness to the previous night's storm. They rode past washouts and piles of debris, dead animals, broken plants. Late in the afternoon they turned toward the road and saw that it was washed bare of tracks. Old wagon ruts still existed, but they were shallower, their edges smoothed. They passed the place where the flash flood had originated, a confluence of gullies that bordered the road, fed water into them through several spouts and drains.

"This would have been a bad place to be last night," Ferguson said.

"I don't even want to think about it," Trask said. He raised a hand and beckoned to Willy Rawlins. "Let's take the road, Willy," he called. "You all follow us."

"Goin' to leave tracks for that Cody feller," Ferguson said.

"I know. Hell, I want him to follow us now. I think Pablo's going to take care of Zak Cody."

"I hope to hell you're right, Ben."

They spoke little as Trask set a faster pace. It was easier going on the road, and he knew he was leaving tracks. Cody would know just how many of them were ahead of him and where they were going. Well, he thought, that was just Cody's bad luck.

The clouds began to break up and drift apart. Some were shredded by high altitude winds and hung like tattered gray curtains from puffy, elongated lintels. Others looked like the foam circling a whirlpool, and these were drifting apart in clumps from the center. Clouds with smudged underbellies turned white as they passed under them, like optical illusions, or perhaps a deception brought on by the constant shift of light as it played over land and sky.

By late afternoon there were only puffs and streamers as reminders of the night before, a few scattered white clouds with little definition and an uncertain destination. The sun was boiling hot and the men were all sweating, griping about the heat. They drank from their canteens and chewed on jerky and hardtack. They smoked and kept riding, their horses striped with sweat, switching their tails at ravenous flies, snorting and wheezing under the grueling pace.

As the sun fell away in the sky, their shadows stretched out in front of them, growing longer and longer. The land itself seemed to change as the shadows pooled up, shapes shifting and reshifting as they rode. Trask kept looking at the road behind him, and every time he did, Grissom and Rawlins did the same. The Mexicans all looked ahead and to the sides, their nerves stretched taut, their horses laboring as they tired and perspired.

Just at dusk, Ferguson raised an arm and pointed ahead.

"There's the next stage stop," he said.

"I see it," Trask said. He turned and made a circling sign with his hand.

Grissom peeled off to the right, Rawlins to the left, leaving the road. They rode in a wide semicircle to flank the adobe.

"Thin out," Trask said to the others. "Don't bunch up. You see anything don't look right, you shoot it."

"Do it, boys," Ferguson said, and the Mexicans fanned out.

Trask slowed his horse. Ferguson did the same.

"Let's see if Willy or Lou run into anything," Trask said.

The sun was sinking below the western horizon now, painting the clouds silver and gold, tinting the undersides with soft orange pastels. The shadows deepened to the east, twisted into formless shapes like clay in the hands of a mad sculptor.

Willy reached the adobe first and circled it on his horse. Lou took an opposite tack on his horse, and the two met out front. Trask reined up and held his hand high to stop the others. They all waited and watched as Willy dismounted and drew his pistol. He crept up to the open door and called out, "Hello the house."

There was no answer.

Then he went inside and Trask held his

breath. He returned a few moments later, stood in the doorway and wig-wagged an arm to signal all clear.

"Let's go, Hiram," Trask said, and motioned for the others to follow.

Lou dismounted and tied his horse to a hitchrail.

"Empty?" Trask said as he rode up.

"Nobody alive in there, if that's what you mean," Willy said.

"Well, anybody dead in there?"

"Ben, it looks like the two men here were blown to bits and what was left of their skins was gnawed off. Just skeletons, mostly, a couple of skulls grinnin' and settin' apart from a lot of bones. Stinks to high heaven."

Ferguson let out a groaning sigh.

Trask looked at him.

"Hiram, you didn't expect no good news here, did you?"

"No, I reckon not. Them were both good boys. I hate to lose 'em."

"Well, you lost 'em and we're ridin' on." He stared at Grissom and Rawlins. "You boys get mounted. We're ridin' on."

"Hell, it'll be dark soon," Grissom said, looking at Ferguson for support. There was none.

"We'll get you a pet owl, Lou. He can be your eyes. We're ridin' on."

"Yeah, damn it all."

"You wouldn't want to stay here no ways, Lou," Rawlins said. "It's worsen the place we stayed in last night. The smell, I mean."

The other riders rode up. Some of them started to dismount. Ferguson put up a hand to stop them.

"We're not bunkin' here tonight, boys," he said. "Trask says we're goin' on." Then he turned to Trask. "It's another day's ride or so to the next station, Ben."

"I know. Just sit tight while I work this out."

Trask touched spurs to his horse's flanks and guided him around the adobe. Behind it, he rode some distance, scouting the terrain. When he returned, the sun was nearly set and the faces of the men were in shadow.

"Pablo," Trask said, "come with me. The rest of you just wait. Roll a quirly, scratch your ass, stretch your legs. But stay close to your horses."

Trask and Medina rode to the back of the adobe and beyond.

"You can tie your horse to that pile of lumber yonder, Pablo. Anyone comin' up the road won't see him. Then you sit in that house and poke your gun barrel out one of the winders. If Cody rides up, he's going to be real close. He'll be wearin' black and ridin' a black horse, like I said. You might drop him at close range. There's a back door. Leave it open, and after you've killed that bastard and maybe the soldier, you hightail it for your horse and light a shuck. You got that?"

"Yes. I will wait inside the adobe for this Cody and shoot him."

"Kill him."

"Yes."

"Maybe you'll get lucky and he won't get here until tomorrow, after the sun is up."

"I have seen dust in the sky," Pablo said. "He is coming. He is near."

"How come you didn't tell me?"

"Sometimes I look and it is there. I look again and it is gone. I think he rides fast and then rides slow. The dust was far away."

"You got good eyes, Pablo. I'm countin' on them tonight. You see good in the dark?"

"Yo soy un tecolote," he said.

"What's that mean?" Trask asked.

"I am the owl."

Trask laughed, reached over and patted Pablo between his shoulder blades.

"You'll do, Pablo. You'll do right fine."

When Trask and the others left, the sun had set and the temperature began dropping.

Pablo squatted by a front window, his

193

Winchester resting on the ledge, the barrel pointing toward the road. It was quiet and dark, the sky sprinkled with diamond stars, the moon not yet risen.

He waited and fought against superstition and fear, his stomach fluttering like a child's on All Hallow's Eve, when the ghosts of the dead floated on the night air and the faintest whisper would make him shiver as if touched by the bony hand of a skeleton.

He waited and thought about the man he was going to kill. The one they called the Shadow Rider.

CHAPTER 20

Zak had not ridden more than ten feet before Colleen caught up to him.

One look at her face and he knew she had the bit in her teeth. This was one woman no man would ever best in an argument. He braced himself for what he suspected would be another angry tirade.

"Zak Cody," she said, lighting into him like a mother hen attacking a hawk in the chicken house, "are you just going to let that dead man lie up there on that hill without a proper burial?"

"Yes, I am," he said. "There's no way to bury him proper."

"Well, you can dig a hole, or cover him with rocks, at least."

"Wouldn't do any good, Colleen. And it would hold us back. We have to move on Trask, stop him from rendezvousing with . . . well, with some renegades who are trying to start a war with the Apache nation."

"Where's your respect for the dead, Zak?"

"I don't respect the dead, I reckon. I respect the living."

"What? I've never heard such a thing. No respect for the dead?"

"No'm."

"That man needs to be buried. By you. By us. Before we leave."

"No'm, he does not."

"Why?"

Zak tried to avoid those penetrating blue eyes of hers, but they were like magnets. They drew his own gaze to them, so he could not avoid mentally plunging into their depths and being snared there like a rabbit in a trap. Her eyes were especially beautiful and magnetic when she was angry. And he was sure that Colleen was hopping mad.

"Be like burying a suit, ma'am."

"What?" Her eyes flared like twin star sapphires struck with a sudden glaring light.

"The man's dead, Colleen. Gone. Nothing more we can do for him. It would be just like burying a man's suit clothes. Senseless."

"Oh, you are really something, Zak Cody. As heartless a man as I've ever met, and I've met my share of them, all right."

"Maybe so," he said.

"Just to leave that poor dead man lying up there, out in the open, subject to the ravages of weather and vermin, all kinds of awful things."

"Yes'm. Nature takes care of such. Mother Nature cleans up the messes we human folks leave. Worms are already at work on him. Flies will get at his eyes, start drinking all the wet stuff. Buzzards will pick at him until the coyotes pick up the scent, and then they'll cart off arms and legs. Ants and bugs will get a share, until there's not much of a trace. His clothes will eventually rot, his pistol turn to rust. That's the way life works, Colleen. Dust to dust."

"Oh, you're impossible, Zak. I expected you'd show a little compassion, a little respect for —"

"Colleen, the Lakota, the Crow, the Cheyenne, maybe all Indian tribes, always thank the spirit of the creatures they kill for food. So do I. The Lakota say this: 'Thank you, brother, for feeding me and my family. One day I will die and feed the grasses so your descendants can eat and live and become strong.' That's the way life works. Everything alive feeds on something else to survive. When we pluck a fruit or a vegetable to eat, we kill it. When we slaughter a beef or shoot a deer, we are living life, the life the Great Spirit gave us."

"People are different," she said. "They deserve some reverence when they die."

"Why? People are just another animal, as far as the Great Spirit is concerned. Oh, we think we're smarter than most animals, but I've seen animals that have more good sense than a lot of men."

"That's not what I'm talking about, Zak."

"Colleen, you haven't seen all of life. Neither have I. But I've seen maybe a great deal more than you have. No death is ever pretty, but it's just a condition that all creatures must experience. The Indians believe that a man's spirit lives in his body while he is alive on this earth. After death, the spirit leaves, goes along the star path to a better place."

"Heaven, you mean."

"You can call it anything you want," he said. "The point is that we are all here on this earth for only a little while. When death takes us, we are no longer here."

"And you believe that?" Her voice had softened, grown less shrill. The light in her eyes was now filled with flitting shadows of doubt.

"Yes, Colleen, I guess I do. Now, we can talk about this later, if you like, but I have a job to do and we're moving on."

"I must say, you do give a person food for thought."

"Thinking can brighten the darkest path, sometimes."

She looked at him as if seeing him for the first time. Her eyes narrowed. Her lips pursed as if she was about to speak, but she pressed them back together and turned her horse away. He did not detect anger, but a kind of puzzlement that she couldn't unravel as long as she was in his presence. A smile flickered on his lips as he touched spurs to his mount's flanks. The horse responded with bunched muscles that suddenly released the energy in its legs and hooves.

The sky grew lighter in color and softer in texture as they rode away from the hill, along a path Zak set, parallel to the washed-out roadway, clouds still hiding the rising sun.

O'Hara caught up with Cody, rode alongside him. He didn't speak for some time and Zak didn't encourage him to talk.

Finally, the lieutenant cleared his throat.

"Prisoner seems to be doing all right," he said.

"We haven't gone far. There should be a stage stop up ahead any minute now."

"What did you say to Colleen?" O'Hara

was blunt, and Zak knew that was what he really wanted to talk about, not Al Deets.

"About what?"

"She seemed pretty upset when we left that Mexican up there on the hill."

"She wanted me to bury him."

"And you refused."

"He's not buried, is he?"

"Colleen, well, she's sensitive, I guess you'd say. Delicate, maybe, in some ways. I just didn't want her feelings hurt. Unnecessarily, I mean."

Zak said nothing. He let Ted chew on that for a while. The way he figured it, if Ted had something more to say, he would say it.

And he did, finally.

"Maybe we should have buried that dead man, Zak."

"You think so? Why?"

"A matter of decency, I guess."

"What would be decent about piling rocks on a rotting corpse?"

"Good lord, Zak, I hope you didn't say anything like that to Colleen."

"I hope I didn't, either," Zak said.

O'Hara frowned.

Zak was watching the land ahead, his gaze scanning the terrain for any sign of movement, any glint of light on a gun barrel. The sunlight had not broken through yet, but it was stronger now, the heavy purple of the far clouds to the east fading to a light lavender, while some were tinged a pale cobalt, and there were signs that the lower clouds were breaking up, swirled into spirals by the lofty winds. The sun would break through eventually, and the dank coolness that clung to the land would vanish as it bathed in scorching heat.

"You must know what you said to Colleen," O'Hara said.

"Some of it. Why?"

"I guess it might not be any of my business."

"It might not," Zak agreed.

"You're a hard man to get to know, Zak. I sure can't figure you out."

"It's not important, Ted. You ought to have more to figure out than me. Like how we're going to bring Ben Trask down and stop a bloody war with the Apaches."

"Oh, I'm thinking about that, sure. Not much we can do right now."

"No. Just make sure Trask and his men don't jump us."

"You think he might? This early in the day?"

"Trask is capable of 'most anything. My guess is that he'll look for a good place to dry-gulch us and start slinging a whole lot of lead our way."

"When?"

"I don't know. Today. Tomorrow, maybe."

Zak stood up in the stirrups. Ahead, on a low rise, he saw the adobe, just jutting up on the edge of his vision.

"There's the old stage stop," he said. "Trask probably holed up there during the storm. He might be there now. Or he might have left a couple of rifles behind to pick us off."

"Hard to see," O'Hara said, squinting. "It looks just like the land around it. Same drab color and all."

"I left two men dead in it last time I was here."

"You did? Trask's men?"

"Trask's or Ferguson's. They were left there to join up with Trask. There were two men at each old stage stop."

"You kill all of them?" There was a hollow sound to O'Hara's voice, as if he were swallowing the words as he spoke them.

"I did."

O'Hara said nothing. Zak reined his horse to a halt.

"You stay here, Ted. Spread out. I'll circle and come up from the left side of that adobe yonder. You keep your eyes on the road to your right."

"You want me to go with you? Maybe one of the men?"

"No. I can tell if there are any surprises waiting for us."

"You're in command, Colonel."

Zak shot him a sharp look, a silent reprimand.

Then he rode on, circling to the left, keeping the horse at a walk so he would not make much noise.

He found the places where Trask had hobbled the horses the night before. He dismounted and broke open the freshest horse apples. No steam arose from the balls of dung. He checked the hoofprints to gauge how old they were, and then, when he had remounted, he rode out, counting tracks, making sure that none doubled back. Then he rode back up behind the adobe and around to the other side. He saw the collapsed wall, the ruins inside. He rode back out front and waved to O'Hara, beckoning him to ride up with Colleen, Deets, and the two soldiers.

Zak dismounted then, checked the front door, looked at the disheveled interior. There was mud inside, along with standing water, debris scattered everywhere.

When Ted rode up with the others, Zak stepped outside.

"What'd you find, Zak?" Ted asked.

"Well, Trask and his bunch spent a miserable night here. They left a good hour or so ahead of us. At this point, he doesn't outnumber us much."

"How many?"

"I counted eight horse tracks, but one of them is traveling empty. Probably belonged to that dead Mexican back there."

"That doesn't sound so bad, then."

"Bad enough. They're all killers and they're riding faster than we are."

"You can tell that from the tracks?"

"I figure they'll let that riderless horse loose when they get far enough away. It will slow them down. And Trask is in a hurry."

"Now what?" Ted wanted to know.

"We follow Trask. But from here on out, he can dry-gulch us most anywhere. I figure that at some point he'll ride down to the road so he can make better time. Along here, the road looks pretty bad. Still muddy, still choked with a lot of dead animals, brush, and such."

O'Hara looked off toward the road, then at the crumbled wall.

"Rain must have damned near drowned them if they were all inside. I wonder why he killed one of his own men."

Zak looked at Deets.

"He might know," he said. "What about it, Deets? Any idea why Trask would shoot that Mexican?"

"No tellin'," Deets said. "He might've looked at Trask crosswise."

"We may never know," Zak said. He started to walk to his horse. "Let's keep moving. There's another old stage stop about a day's ride from here. Trask might hole up there tonight."

"You think so?" O'Hara asked.

"I echo Deets there. No telling what Trask might do, but he'll go there to see if the two men they put there are still alive."

O'Hara looked at Colleen as Zak climbed back up in the saddle.

A knowing look spread across her face.

"He won't find them alive, will he, Zak?" she said.

"Not unless they've been resurrected. I only know of one such case of that."

"You're not only crass and heartless," she said, "you're also sacrilegious, Zak Cody."

"I wish you'd quit calling me by both my names," he said. "You make me think of my mother when she was mad at me."

"Well, I'm not your mother, but you do make me mad."

O'Hara opened his mouth to say something, but wisely kept silent.

"Thank God for that," Zak said with a wry smile. He turned his horse and rode up the slope to where Trask's trail began.

Behind him, Zak heard Colleen give out an indignant snort.

And he smiled again.

CHAPTER 21

Zak rode well ahead of the others, following the tracks of Trask's bunch. The others stopped a few times so that Colleen, her brother, Deets, Scofield, and Rivers could heed calls to nature. Colleen, of course, took longer than the others. Zak stopped to relieve himself a few times, too. They all had to use precious water to wash their hands. Ted guarded his sister when she was occupied with those private tasks, staying at a discreet distance, his rifle at the ready.

Zak came across a saddle, saw where Trask and the others had stopped to strip it from the riderless horse. A few yards away he saw a discarded bridle. Attached to the saddle was an empty rifle scabbard, which he did not examine. He saw the tracks left by the horse the outlaws shooed away. He scanned the terrain all around but saw no sign of the abandoned horse.

A while later the tracks left the rough

country and joined the road. Zak saw that all of the riders moved much faster over the washed-out road. There were clumps of mud thrown up by the horses' hooves when they rode at a gallop. He dismounted and broke open a few mud balls to gauge how old they were. Trask, he figured, was now at least two hours ahead of them, perhaps more.

When he reached the road, he stopped and waited for O'Hara and the others to join him.

"So," Ted said, "Trask is taking to the road."

"And picking up the pace. He's a good two hours ahead of us, maybe three. More like three, I'd say."

"That's a good long stretch," O'Hara said.

"We can't make it up, for sure. We have to spare our horses. Look at that sky. By mid-afternoon we'll be sweating rivers."

O'Hara looked up at the sky, saw the swirls of decimated clouds, the basking loaves floating on separate seas of blue, the grated remnants of white carpets floating in the high ether. The sun was blinding by then, coursing slow and blazing toward its noon zenith.

"No way to catch him before he meets up with Welch, I suppose," O'Hara said.

"There might be a way," Zak said.

"How?"

"If we stop less, sleep on our horses. Trask may hole up in one of those adobe line shacks for some shut-eye. If so, we gain on him."

"None of us got any sleep last night, Zak."

"I know. We've got three or four days of hard riding ahead of us. We might go three days without sleep. After that, we'll start to fall off our horses, make mistakes, maybe get all mixed up on time and directions."

"You paint a pretty grim picture," O'Hara said.

"Grim, not pretty."

O'Hara laughed at the wry observation. "I guess we can try," he said. "I've slept in the saddle before."

"It's your sister I'm worried about, Ted."

"Colleen? She's holding up well so far. I can keep an eye on her, so she doesn't tumble out of the saddle."

"You might have Rivers or Scofield do that. I may need your eyes and your rifle before this day is done."

"I understand."

"I'm going to have Deets ride with me from now on."

"Your decoy?"

"He won't be any big loss if he takes a bullet."

"You expect that will happen?"

"I don't know what to expect. But if we are shot at — if Deets is shot at — it might give me the split second I need to shoot back."

"Sound reasoning, Zak."

Zak laughed. "I don't know how sound it is. I'm just trying to give us a chance if Trask is waiting up ahead to pick us off. We're outgunned, Ted."

"Is there anything else we can do? Maybe go to the fort and put Willoughby in irons, get together a troop to go after Trask, Ferguson, and Welch?"

"That would eat up days we don't have," Zak said.

O'Hara thought about it for a minute or so. There wasn't a hint of a breeze, and the sun was bearing down on them with molten persistence. Sweat began to trickle out from under his hat and he swiped at it with his hand.

"What would General Crook do, Zak?"

"Good question."

"Do you know the answer?"

O'Hara, Zak thought, was as persistent as a wood tick. Once he landed on live meat, he burrowed right into it.

"Crook would rest his troops before he went into battle."

"Then there's your answer."

"You're right, Ted. General Crook would also pick his own battlefield."

"Your point, Zak?"

"We can do that. We know where Trask is going. And we know where Cochise is."

"So, what's your decision?" Ted asked.

"I'll let you know at the end of the day."

"Why then?"

"Because I hope to make it to the next adobe. What I find there will tell me what to do."

"Fair enough. I hope you make the right decision."

"Every decision is the right one," Zak said. "At the time you make it. You only know if it's wrong if it turns out to be a bad decision."

They followed the tracks up the road, with Deets riding alongside Zak, the others following some hundred yards in the rear.

"I feel wet inside," Deets said to Zak sometime after noon.

"You've been drinking too much water."

"No, I mean where your bullet went through me, Cody."

"You're probably bleeding again. Put your

211

hand on the wound and press hard. Keep it there."

"I touched it a minute ago. Burns like fire."

"Bleed to death, then, Deets."

"Damn, Cody. I'm hurtin', I tell you."

"If you feel pain, that's a good sign, Deets."

"What about the bleeding?"

"That, too, is a good sign."

"A good sign?"

Zak decided that Deets wasn't too bright. And he obviously wasn't a leader. He was a follower.

"Yeah, Deets. If you hurt and you're bleeding, that's a sign you're still alive. Give thanks to your Maker, son."

"You bastard."

"Your mouth works all right, too. Maybe tonight I'll build a fire and put some iron to that wound, seal it up. And maybe wash your mouth out with some lava soap."

"We gonna stop somewheres?"

Zak didn't answer. He studied the tracks, getting a picture of Trask's tactics from the sign. Trask and his men would walk their horses for a good stretch, three or four miles, then gallop them for nearly a mile. He was unwavering in that maneuver. But he noticed that some of the horses were starting to drag their hooves, a sure sign of fatigue.

As the day wore on, Trask no longer ran the horses, but kept to a steady, plodding pace. He seemed pretty confident, Zak thought. And Zak noticed that two horses had paired up for a time, then one went ahead, leaving the other behind. After that, the horses all stuck to their positions. When they stopped, it was only briefly, to relieve themselves, and always, two riders stood off from the others, probably to stand guard until they took their turns. The doodle bug holes marked both their passing and their activities.

Zak could see that Trask was thorough, and smart. It was what made him dangerous.

Later, he thought about Crook and something the general had told him once, when they were fighting Indians, tracking a band that had escaped a battle in rugged country.

"You have to think like your enemy, Zak," Crook had told him. "When you're on his track, you have to see ahead of him, think what he might do, what you might do if you were in his shoes, or his moccasins."

"Can you do that, General?"

"Any animal will only run so far. Then it gets tired or mad and makes a stand. But the animal always picks the place to make a stand. If you're chasing that animal, you have to think like it thinks. Where would it make its stand? How would it defend itself? In the case of these redskins, they'll find high ground with plenty of cover. And they'll have a back door, a place where they can run and escape if they fail to stop me."

"And do you know where that is?"

"No, but I will. And so will you. That's why you're my scout, Zak. You can read sign and you can read what those redskins are thinking. Am I right?"

"Yes, sir, I reckon you are."

And Zak had figured out where the Indians were going and where they would halt and make a stand. Crook acted accordingly and they killed or captured the entire band. Crook was a good general. He knew when to delegate authority and how to do it. Not a bad example to follow, Zak thought.

The sun drifted down the arch of the western sky, hovered over the horizon, then started dipping beyond it, striping the land with shadows, painting clouds gold and silver, purple and a soft orange. Zak called a halt while it was still light enough to see everyone with him and the terrain ahead.

He beckoned to O'Hara and the others to catch up to him and Deets, then waited.

When they were all there, gathered around him, he spoke.

"We're not too far from the next old stage stop," he said. "I notice that Trask's horses are tired, so he and his men must be tired."

"And so are we, Mr. Cody," Colleen said, a sharp tone to her voice.

"We may not be able to see that adobe right off, especially if it's real dark, so stay alert. If Trask is holed up there, he probably won't light a fire, and he'll try and be real quiet. When I see the shack, I'll call a halt and deploy you all until I find out if the adobe is occupied. From now on you'll ride close behind me and Deets. Lieutenant O'Hara, you'll take the lead. Scofield, you and Rivers will flank Miss O'Hara. Check your rifles. Keep them at the ready."

"How far is that adobe?" Ted asked.

"Maybe less than ten miles. We've kept a pretty good pace, but the tracks tell me Trask is probably just about there, or will be shortly after sunset. So, we've got a good two hours ride, maybe longer, before we know anything."

"Lead on, Zak," O'Hara said. "The quicker we get there, the better."

"Maybe," Zak said, and turned his horse, motioned for Deets to follow him.

Three quarters of an hour later the sun

set below the horizon. The afterglow lingered for another fifteen or twenty minutes, a last blaze against the western clouds as those ahead of them turned to ash, then to ebony, before they disappeared.

As they rode on, Venus winked on in an aquamarine sky and the darkness crept across the heavens, leaving more stars, like scattered diamonds, on black velvet.

Zak tried to recall the exact location of the stage stop that had been turned into a line shack before its abandonment. The darkness didn't help, although he had passed this same way a few days ago on just such a night.

Deets was making noises, groaning, muttering under his breath.

"Shut up," Zak told him in a loud whisper. "You make any more noise and I'll stuff a rag in your mouth."

Deets shut up.

Another hour passed and the darkness deepened.

The moon rose and Zak got his bearings. He pulled on the reins and halted the horse he was riding, Deets's horse. The others caught up to him.

He kept his voice low when he spoke to them.

"The old line shack's just head. Maybe

five hundred yards. Keep Deets here. I'm going to dismount and proceed on foot. If you hear a shot, wait five minutes before you circle the adobe on horseback. If I don't come back in five minutes, I probably won't be back."

"Want me to go with you?" O'Hara asked.

"No, I'll go this one alone. I have a funny feeling in my stomach. And I always pay attention to funny feelings."

"What do you think?"

"I don't know. If Trask and his men are up there, we should hear some noises. Faint noises, maybe, but some sounds. Sounds of life. He may not be there. Or there might be one or a bunch up there, just waiting for anyone to come up on that adobe from this road."

"Be careful," Colleen said, and Zak felt the softness in her voice, the concern she expressed. He swung out of the saddle and drew his rifle from its sheath.

He handed the reins of the horse to Ted.

"I'll be seeing you," he said.

Then he walked a few paces and disappeared into the darkness.

CHAPTER 22

Major Erskine Willoughby studied the map that lay on top of his desk. An oil lamp flickered with a yellow-orange flame, spraying a wavering light over the lines and boxes, the X's and circles, the numbers and letters. He tapped an impatient foot against one leg of his chair, creating a rhythmic tattoo that served to calm his clamorous nerves.

"Orderly," he called through the closed door, "where in hell is Lieutenant Welch?"

"He's coming, sir," a voice replied, warped by the wood barrier through which it traveled. "Corporal Hopson ran to fetch him ten minutes ago."

"As you were," Willoughby said, gaining some equilibrium with his thoughts in issuing a meaningless order. Of course the orderly would be as he was. Willoughby couldn't see him through the door, but he knew the man was standing stiff as a board, as apprehensive as he himself would be until Lieutenant Welch appeared.

Fort Bowie was on the map. The cartographer had drawn a line from the fort to the last old stage stop. The road from Tucson to all the adobes was indicated, as well as the domain of the Chiricahua Apaches. There were little lines drawn in circular fashion to indicate prominent hills all through the area designated as Apache Territory.

Willoughby had studied the map intensely, figuring distances, time of travel by horseback, the rendezvous point with Ferguson, and possible logistical sites should there be a need to reinforce the men or resupply them with food and ammunition, fresh horses, and water.

He loved every minute of the planning. Willoughby not only saw himself as a great general someday, but as a man of property, of immense wealth. He could imagine becoming a land baron on the largely unsettled frontier. And not only would he be an owner of vast acreage, but he would found a town, establish a bank and mercantile store, be wealthy and respected by all who came to settle in what once had been a wild and dangerous country populated by savage Indians.

These were his dreams, and he lived them

each time he studied the map and made notations on a separate piece of paper. Perhaps the army was content to live in peace with the Apaches, but he was not. As long as there were Apaches in the territory, his dreams were in danger of being shattered or never coming to fruition.

Willoughby scratched more notes on the piece of foolscap next to the map. He scribbled each word with an intense focus, picturing himself as a military genius whose strategies would one day be studied by hordes of students attending the academy at West Point. He was so absorbed in this task that he did not hear the discreet knock on his door until after his orderly had rapped on the wood several times.

"Yes?" he said.

"Lieutenant Welch, sir. He has arrived."

"Send him in, Corporal Loomis."

The door opened. John Welch strode into the room, a leather map case tucked under his left arm. He saluted smartly before Loomis closed the door behind him. Willoughby, who was uncovered, did not return his salute.

"Come on over, Johnny. We'll go over this map one more time. You bring yours?"

"Yes, Erskine, of course. I made some notations on it, as you suggested."

"Spread it out here."

Willoughby slid his map and note paper to one side, leaving a space for Welch to place his map of the same terrain. When Welch was finished placing weights on the four corners, Willoughby leaned over the desk and studied it, a series of "Uh-hums" issuing from his throat. Welch glanced over at Willoughby's map to compare the two, but the major blocked most of the light so he could not tell much.

"Very good, Johnny," Willoughby said. "I've got some ideas that might help you in this campaign. How many men have you got so far, and were you able to obtain clothing for them?"

"I've got twenty-five men, eight from the stockade. The rest are family conscripts."

"Family conscripts?"

"Men whose families forced them to join the army. They fucked up at every post and were sent out here for disciplinary reasons. Ain't a one of 'em what's not thoroughly expendable."

Willoughby smiled.

"Good, good."

"All will be wearing civilian clothing, which I obtained from Ferguson. His man rode in from Tucson less than an hour ago. Ferguson and Trask left three days ago. I figure we can rendezvous with them sometime tomorrow afternoon at that last old station."

"About how we figured it, right?"

"Right on the money; right on the barrelhead, Erskine."

"Weaponry?"

"Spencer rifles, forty rounds per man, extra horses, grub for a week."

"I want this done right, Johnny."

Welch was an officious officer, prim as a martinet, stiff-backed, army regulation all the way. He stood at attention even when relaxed. The army was his life, but he was as greedy as Willoughby, and twice as dishonest. He bore a thin black moustache, flared sideburns an inch short of being overly ostentatious, and a uniform so starched and pressed it appeared brand new. But he was the quartermaster. He could get anything he wanted, from almost anywhere.

"The men don't know where they're going, and they won't until we're well away from the fort. They've been told that they will all be granted honorable discharges from the army upon completion of this expedition."

"What do they think this expedition is all about?" Willoughby asked.

Welch smiled. "They think they're going

on a hunt for Apache artifacts to be sent back to a museum in Washington, D.C. They believe the expedition is at the request of our President, Ulysses S. Grant."

"Very good, Johnny. Inspired."

"Yes, sir, I thought so."

"And you'll tell them to kill Apaches."

"Once we're well into the field, sir."

"When do you leave?"

"Shortly after midnight, I'll give the orders. We should be moving before two A.M. At daylight, or shortly thereafter, I'll break the news to the troops that we're going to start a war with the Chiricahua Apaches."

Willoughby stood up. He rolled up his map, placed it atop Welch's on one edge and rolled his map inside the other one. He handed the roll to Welch, then opened the humidor on his desk. He took out two cigars, handed one to the lieutenant.

"I'll see you back here in about a week, minus a few of those miscreants who are going with you, I hope."

"Yes, sir. I'll be coming back with Ferguson and Trask. Just the two of them, sir."

"There won't be any trace of this, ah, expedition, then?"

"No, Erskine, not a goddamned trace."

Willoughby lifted the chimney on the oil

lamp, thrust a taper inside until it caught fire. He lighted Welch's cigar, then his own. He blew a plume of smoke into the air, patted his flat stomach and sat down in his chair.

"Have a seat, Johnny," Willoughby said, "this might be the last good smoke we'll have together for a whole week."

Welch sat down, puffed on his cigar.

"It's going to be sweet, when it's over, Erskine," he said.

"It damned well better be. Our futures depend on this mission."

"The world will be a better place out here when we finish the job."

"You know we have to kill those two men when you bring them back here," Willoughby said.

"Sir?"

"Ferguson and Trask. They will be found guilty of murder and hanged. We can't have them sticking their fingers into our pie."

"No, sir, we can't."

"I want you to bring evidence back with you that they shot two of my soldiers. Can you do that?"

Welch didn't even have to think about it.

"I can, Erskine. You know I can."

Willoughby smiled, blew a smoke ring. It hung in the air like the ghost of a doughnut, wafted across his desk and vanished in a golden spray of lamplight.

The wood inside the room ticked like a clock in the silence.

CHAPTER 23

Zak stepped into the shadows. He became a shadow. Behind him, he heard Colleen let out a tiny gasp. Then he heard someone else draw in a quick breath. Then the silence of the night enveloped him and he circled below the adobe to come up on its north side. He could see only the roof, barely visible in the starlight, the moon just beginning to rise, far to the east.

He stood still for a few moments, almost willing his eyes to adjust to the darkest regions ahead of him. He waited, listened, glad that the horses were quiet. So, too, his ears adjusted to that silence, and he thought of them as small cushions that would absorb every slight noise so he could interpret their origins. Soft, cushiony sponges, soaking up the stillness, adjusting, constantly adjusting, to every nuance of sound the night might have to offer.

He took a step, a careful step, short

enough so he could keep his balance. He did not move the other foot until the first one had settled. He did not disturb the small pebbles nor dislodge the larger rocks, but sought out the open sandy spots where he might place a boot without making a sound.

He took his time, and after a while reached a place parallel to the north wall of the adobe. He approached it with careful steps, watching for anything growing, since he did not want his trouser legs to brush against leaves or bark or cactus. He reached the wall and pressed an ear against it and stood there for several long moments, listening for the scrape of a boot, the clearing of a throat, the shifting of a body in waiting.

He eased himself to the front corner, again pressed his ear to the adobe brick, holding his breath, listening with the intensity of an owl listening for the cheep of a chick or the squeak of a mouse.

He heard a slight scraping sound.

Very slight.

What was it? A rodent inside the shack? A snake slithering across something on the floor? He waited, ear hugging the wall.

Or a man?

He tried to think about what position a man inside might take if he were on guard, waiting to catch some unsuspecting riders coming up on him. He would stand or sit near a window or an open door. He would have a rifle, so he might be at a window, resting the barrel on the sill. He would be looking toward the road, ready to crack off a shot at anyone who approached.

Such a man might have been waiting inside for a long time. Many hours. He might be tired, or sleepy. He might have to change his position often to avoid fatigue. Such a man would be patient.

As Zak was patient now.

There had been no sound for several seconds. The seconds became minutes and passed. Still, Zak stood there, listening, feeling the weight of his rifle as it rested on his forearm, feeling the weight of it grow into a leaden burden. He did not move. He brushed away the thought of that particular discomfort. He made the weight go away until there was a numbness in that spot where the barrel rested, until his hand on the stock felt no weight.

Then he heard a louder noise. A scraping sound, then a sound like metal striking wood, sharp and quick. More scraping sounds and one that was difficult to define. A light stomping sound as if a man was lifting up one foot, then the other, perhaps restoring blood circulation to deadened feet. A perfectly natural thing to do, Zak thought. If a man had been squatting or sitting for some time, perhaps several hours, he would have to stand up, stretch. If he had a rifle in his hands, that rifle might fall to the sill or on a board and make one of the sounds he had heard.

He took his ear away from the wall, rubbed it to bring the blood back into the squashed parts.

He stepped around the corner, hugging the wall. He did not need to put his ear to the wall. He saw that the window on his side was open. He heard the rustle of cloth.

Was there one man inside? Or two? Trask's whole bunch was certainly not inside. That many men would make a lot more noise than he had heard. Most likely one, he thought.

The sounds stopped then, and he knew the man was no longer lifting his boots. Instead, there was a rustle of cloth as the man turned or flexed his arms. It was a sound that was hard to detect, but unmistakable to Zak. He could picture the man standing there, perhaps at the window on the other side of the door. He stretched his neck out and saw that the door was closed.

He moved toward it, a slow, careful step

at a time. When he reached it, he did not lean against it, but stood there. He craned his neck again and saw what he had expected to see.

The other window was open, also, and the dark snout of a rifle rested on the sill, ten or twelve inches poking out.

One lone man, then, as he'd thought.

Who would Trask leave behind? he wondered.

A crack shot, for one thing.

Trask would tell his man to look for a man dressed in black riding a black horse. He would probably trust this man to do the job of assassination. Well, Zak thought, perhaps trust was the wrong word. He would expect the man to carry out his assignment. Perhaps he offered bonus money. Bounty money.

He looked at the door. He traced a finger along the crack. The door was closed tightly, but if he remembered correctly, the doors on these old shacks used leather hinges. Over the years, the leather had probably started to rot or lose its toughness. There might be a latch or a bar on the other side. It might be too risky to knock down the door, crash it open, rush inside and hope he got the waiting killer with his first shot.

But they could not stay there all night.

Something had to be done.

Again Zak's thoughts turned to Trask and which of his men he might have left behind. He might not leave someone he'd known for some time. Too dangerous. He might leave one of Ferguson's men, perhaps one of the Mexicans.

More likely, Trask would do that. Risk someone he did not know too well or might need for the big job ahead.

So there could be a Mexican inside.

Zak set his rifle down behind him, leaned it against the wall. It was not cocked, and if he had to cock it, that would alert the man inside the adobe, give him the advantage.

He drew his pistol, easing it up out of its holster with a practiced slowness. He thumbed the trigger back while gently squeezing the trigger so it would not click when it was fully cocked.

The locking sear might make a small sound, but nothing loud. No more than a muffled *snick,* at best.

He cocked the pistol, held it at the ready. He listened to see if the slight sound had caused any alarm to the man inside.

It was very quiet.

His next move, he knew, would be the most crucial one.

Zak leaned toward the open window and

whispered.

"*¿Quien es?*" Who's there? in Spanish.

He heard a sucking of breath, the scrape of a boot.

"*¿Quien es?*" the man inside hissed in a loud whisper.

Zak thought fast. He knew now that he had been right. There was a Mexican on guard. His accent was perfect for a man who spoke Spanish. He picked a common Mexican name, hoped that would confuse the man inside. No, he thought, he would use the name of the man they had found shot in the back during the flash flood. He tried to remember his name. "*Es Jaime,*" he said.

He heard the man inside curse under his breath. He murmured the names of saints and invoked Jesus, Mary, and God, all in Spanish.

"*¿Tu no eres muerto, Jaime?*" Pablo Medina said.

Zak saw the rifle barrel disappear, then reappear.

"*Yo soy el espirito de Jaime Elizondo. Soy muerto. Dame agua, dame pan.*" Give me water, give me bread.

"*Jesús Cristo,*" Pablo exclaimed. "*Vete, vete.*"

"*Tira su rifle afuera,*" Zak said. Throw your rifle outside.

"*¿Por qué?*" the man inside said. Why? in Spanish.

In Spanish, Zak replied. At the same time, he kept his eye on the man's rifle, measured the number of strides it would take to reach it, snatch it out of the would-be killer's hands.

"I am the ghost of Jaime Elizondo. I am looking for the man who shot me in the back. I am going to kill that man so I can be free of this earth."

"I did not kill you. Ben Trask shot you, Jaime. Go. Go away."

That was enough for Zak.

He took two long strides, leaping past the door, pouncing downward. With his left hand, he grabbed the rifle barrel, jerked it hard. The man inside held onto it, cried out, then released his hold on it.

Zak flung the rifle away from him like a man would throw a stick to a dog, then rose to a crouch and fired his pistol through the window at pointblank range.

Orange flame spouted from the barrel. The pistol bucked in his hand.

For one terrible moment all time stood still. The deafening roar in Zak's ears blotted out all other sounds. He seemed rooted to that spot where he crouched like a leopard, frozen there for an eternity, not knowing whether his bullet had struck the man at the window or if the next shot would come from that man's pistol and blow his own heart to a bloody pulp.

For that split second of infinity, he did not know whether he would live or die.

He just did not know.

CHAPTER 24

The man inside the adobe cried out. Zak climbed through the open window, cocking his pistol as he cleared the sill. In the flash from his pistol, he had caught just a quick glimpse of the man; not in that instant he had fired, but a second later, when the afterimage registered on his brain.

He was taking a chance, he knew, but also knew he had the advantage. He seized the moment, shoved the man backward, swung his pistol next to the man's head and squeezed the trigger. The explosion reverberated inside the adobe. The man screamed as the concussion shattered his eardrums. Zak saw him clearly in the bright orange flame that erupted from his barrel. He smashed the butt of his pistol into the man's temple, and he dropped like a twenty-pound sash weight, stunned.

Zak pounced on him, pinned him to the littered floor. He put the muzzle of his gun square at the man's temple, waited a second, then cocked the hammer back. There was a loud click, and the man beneath him stiffened in fear.

"*¿Como te llamas?*" Zak asked.

"*M-Me llamo Pablo Medina. ¿Quien eres tu?*"

"I'm the Shadow Rider," Zak said, in Spanish. "I am the man Ben Trask wanted you to kill."

Zak heard hoofbeats and voices. He remembered that he had told Ted to come looking for him if he heard a shot. Ted had heard two shots, and Zak knew he must be wondering what had happened. The voices grew louder, and he heard Colleen's voice and Scofield's. He could not decipher what they were saying to one another. In a few moments the sound of hoofbeats separated and he figured Rivers and Scofield were flanking the adobe, perhaps covering the closed door.

"Zak?" O'Hara called out.

"In here," Zak replied. "Come on in."

A moment later the door opened and the shadow of a man filled the doorway. Ted O'Hara stood there, rifle in hand. Zak heard more hoofbeats, the creaking of leather as people dismounted outside.

"Zak?"

"Down here. I've got a prisoner," Zak said. "There should be a stove or a fireplace in here. Let's have some light."

"Right," O'Hara said.

Pablo Medina struggled to free himself, rolling from side to side, pushing upward with his torso. Zak exerted more pressure on the man's face with his arm. Medina stopped struggling.

O'Hara issued orders from the doorway.

"Rivers, bring Deets in here. Scofield, you stand guard outside. Colleen, come in and help me get a fire going."

O'Hara crashed around the room, feeling his way. Zak heard a clank and a rattle of wood that sounded like loose kindling. A moment later he heard crumpling paper. Rivers and Deets came in after tying up their horses. Colleen followed right after.

"I can't see," she said.

"Just walk toward the sound of my voice, Colleen," O'Hara said. "Be careful. There's stuff on the floor."

Then more sounds as O'Hara stuffed kindling and newspapers into the potbellied stove. He struck a match, and Zak saw the outlines of Medina's face, his black eyes staring up at him in terror.

"I do not want to die," Medina said, in English.

Colleen paused and looked down at Zak's prisoner.

"Did you shoot him?" she asked Zak.

"Help your brother," he said.

She snorted and walked toward her squatting brother and the stove.

The paper caught fire and then the wood started to burn. There was enough light now for Zak to see around the room.

"There's an awful smell in here," Colleen said. "And the place is filthy."

"Find a broom," Ted said to her. "Be careful where you step. There are human remains in here, sis."

Colleen gasped.

Zak spoke to Medina. "Are you hurt?"

"No."

"I'm going to let you up, after I take your pistol from you. If you try to run, I will shoot you dead. Do you understand?"

"Yes."

Zak slipped the pistol from Medina's holster, handed it to Rivers. Then he stood up. He reached down and helped Medina to his feet.

The fire was brighter by then, and threw large shadows on the walls of the adobe. Colleen gasped when she saw the mess inside the shack. She looked around for a broom and a shovel, while Rivers took Deets over to a corner so he would be out of the way.

O'Hara walked over to Zak, who still had a gun on Medina.

"What are you going to do with this man?" he asked.

"Probably let him go," Zak said.

"Let him go?"

"First, a few questions for Pablo here."

Medina blinked both eyes. Then he looked over at Deets, who was still wearing the black slicker and Zak's black hat, then looked again at Zak.

"Yes, that's Al Deets," Zak said to Medina. "If you had seen us ride up in daylight, you'd probably have shot him instead of me, eh, Pablo?"

"It is possible," Medina said in Spanish.

"Speak English," Zak ordered. "How long ago did Trask leave here?"

"I do not know."

Zak poked the barrel of his pistol into Medina's gut, just above the belt buckle. "Drop your gun belt," he said.

Medina unbuckled his belt, let it and the empty holster fall to the floor.

"Now, answer my question, Pablo."

Medina shrugged. "An hour, maybe two."

"He left longer ago than that. Sunset? Just after sunset?"

"Maybe."

Zak lowered his pistol and placed the barrel an inch from Medina's genitals.

Medina flinched. One of his eyes flickered as the skin over his cheekbone twitched.

"I'll blow your *juevos* clean off if you don't give me a straight answer, Pablo."

"After sunset. Maybe three hours ago."

"Zak," O'Hara said, "you know damned well how long ago Trask lit out of here. You can read tracks like I can read an army map."

Zak smiled.

Understanding flickered in Medina's eyes.

"That is true, Ted. So now I know that Pablo can lie, and he knows that I do not lie. Isn't that right, Pablo?"

"Yes. Three hours go by. I wait here."

"Would you like to catch up to Ferguson? You work for him, don't you?"

"I work for Mr. Ferguson. Yes. I would like to go to him."

"Surely, you're not going to let this man go, Zak." O'Hara said. "He'll tell Trask and Ferguson how many men we have and that my sister is with us. Trask would have us at a disadvantage."

Zak watched Pablo Medina's eyes. They pulsed like gelatinous jewels.

Zak smiled without showing his teeth. Just

a flicker of his lips told of his amusement at his prisoner's reactions.

Colleen swept debris into a pile near the door. Then she leaned the broom against the wall, walked back to a place just behind the stove, pulled a shovel off the wall and carried it to the front door. There, she shoveled the debris up and walked outside. Before she left, she looked at Zak.

"I understand Spanish," she said. "I know what you threatened to do to Pablo."

"Pablo understands Spanish, too, Colleen. He knew I would do what I said I would do to him if he didn't talk."

Colleen went outside. Zak heard her toss the debris onto the ground.

He turned back to Ted O'Hara.

"I'm thinking of letting both Deets and Medina here go," he said. "We're not equipped to handle these prisoners."

"That would be a big mistake, Zak."

"If we take on any more prisoners, we'll be outnumbered," Zak said. "We're already short on guards for these two."

"Still, these men would give Trask valuable information. Information he could use against us when we meet up with him."

"I'm not worried about Trask at this point," Zak said.

"You're not?"

"No. He knows I'm on his trail. He thinks Deets is dead, probably. When Pablo here doesn't show up, he'll figure he's dead, too. That won't worry him any. That's why he left this man behind. He doesn't care, but if there was a chance Pablo could kill me, he'd have one less worry."

"So, you're just going to let these men go back to Trask and blab all they know."

"I could cut out their tongues," Zak said, just as Colleen came back inside.

She stopped, stared at Zak with a look of horror on her face.

"You wouldn't . . ." she said.

"There's probably a pair of pliers or some blacksmith's snips in here," he said. "I could either cut off their tongues or jerk them out by the roots."

"You — You're a savage, Zak Cody. A cruel, heartless savage."

"Yes'm," Zak said.

Medina shrank away from him.

"I know you're joking, Zak," O'Hara said. "But I hope you reconsider about turning these two men loose to run off to join Trask."

"I'll let you know my thinking in a while, Ted. First, I want to question Pablo here a little more. You can call Scofield back in

242

here. Nobody's going to ride up on us to-night."

"You're sure?"

"I'm sure. What's more, we're going to spend the night here. We all need sleep. I'll post guards."

"This place is filthy," Colleen said again.

"You'll welcome the rest," Zak told her. "We'll help you clean this place out."

O'Hara walked to the door, called to Scofield, "Come on, Corporal. You're relieved."

"Yes, sir," Scofield said, and after tying his horse to the hitchrail, he entered the adobe.

"You relieve Rivers guarding the prisoner, Scofield," Zak said. "Rivers, you help Colleen shovel out what she sweeps up."

"Yes, sir," Rivers said as Scofield walked back to relieve him.

Zak holstered his pistol after easing the hammer back down. He took Medina by the arm, led him over to the wall next to Deets.

"Sit down," he said. "You, too, Deets."

The two men sat down.

"Scofield, shoot them if they try to get up."

"Yes, sir," Scofield said.

Zak walked back to O'Hara.

"Let's go outside and talk, Ted. I'll tell you why I'm going to let these two men go tell all they know to Trask."

"I can't wait."

The two men walked out into the night. The moon was up a few degrees above the horizon and cast a soft silvery light over the adobe and the surrounding countryside. When they were out of earshot of those inside, Zak stopped. O'Hara stood next to him, waiting to hear what he had to say.

"Nice night," Zak said.

"Are you going to tell me your plans, Zak?"

"No, Ted, I'm not. But those two prisoners in there will think I am. By the time they catch up to Trask, they'll each have a different story. And each one will embellish their stories to suit themselves."

"That's taking a long dubious chance, if you ask me. You don't even have a plan, do you, Zak?"

"Oh, I have a plan all right, Ted. And you'll see signs of it as we continue on after a good night's sleep."

"Signs of it?"

"You don't need to know everything just yet. Better if you don't, in fact. You might be recaptured by Trask, you know."

"Not if you don't let those two men —"

"I'll give the orders here, Lieutenant," Zak said. "You just watch and wait."

O'Hara shook his head. He was puzzled and showed it. Zak said nothing. He looked up at the starry sky and breathed deep of the air. Rivers came to the door a few times and threw out shovels of dirt and debris from the adobe. In the distance, a coyote yipped and then a chorus of yowling canines sang their plaintive songs, ribbons of music floating on the night air.

O'Hara shivered at the sound. "Coyotes give me the willies," he said.

"Coyotes," Zak said. "Or maybe Chiricahua, sounding like coyotes."

O'Hara's eyes narrowed as Zak let a shadowy smile ripple through his lips, his dark eyes bright with moonlight.

CHAPTER 25

Zak worked out the hours in his head.

After retrieving his hat and slicker from Deets, he ordered Scofield to bind the hands and feet of both Medina and Deets. Zak took the first two-hour watch. He found Medina's horse where the man had said it would be, led it back to the adobe and hitched it to the rail with all the others. Then he took a torch down to the road and examined the tracks left by Trask, Ferguson, and the other men in their bunch.

He figured that by the time he arrived at the adobe, Trask had been gone for at least four hours. He knew the outlaws wouldn't last the night before they'd have to stop and get some sleep. And he figured they'd sleep at least three hours, perhaps four. No more than that.

At that pace, Trask would reach the last stage stop sometime in late afternoon. Certainly while there was plenty of daylight left. Welch should be there waiting for him. If not, he'd surely be there shortly afterward. They would study O'Hara's map, plan their campaign against Cochise and the Chiricahuas that night, leave the next morning.

That was the way Zak figured it, and he knew that his calculations could not be far off.

That gave him plenty of time to do what had to be done.

His own campaign against Trask, Ferguson, Welch, and their war party would begin early in the morning. And by the time he turned Deets and Medina loose, they'd have a long ride to rendezvous with Trask.

He was betting they'd never make it. Trask would be long gone by the time Deets and Medina reached that last adobe shack.

Zak rode a wide circle in the moonlight, picking his way with care, noting the landmarks, crossing and recrossing the road. He marked the moon's progress as it rose in the sky and painted the edges of cactus a dull pewter, daubed silver into wet muddy low spots, and glazed the rocks with a misty gray-black patina that made them shift shapes as he passed. It was cool, but not so much that he'd have to don his light jacket, tucked away in a saddlebag. He chewed on dry hardtack and strips of jerked beef, washed the food down with water from his canteen.

He loved the far lonely places, and as he rode, he felt grateful to the Great Spirit for giving him this peaceful night under a canopy of bright stars, whose clusters seemed at times like the lights of distant cities. The Milky Way, the fabled Star Path of the Lakota and the Cheyenne, blazed a brilliant trail across the heavens, more stars than the sands on all the shores of the world.

When he rode back to the adobe at the end of two hours, he felt rich and alive, his plans set in his mind. And he felt that great peace upon him that he always felt when he was outdoors, all alone, contemplating the vastness of the universe, the complexity of all life and all things.

Hugo Rivers was awake and waiting for him when Zak rode up to the hitchrail and dismounted.

"I hereby relieve you, sir," Rivers said in a soft whisper. "Everybody's asleep. Any orders?"

"Just ride a wide circle, no more than a hundred yards from the shack at any time. Figure two hours, then Scofield will take the next watch."

"Yes sir. And, sir?"

"What is it, Rivers?"

"I believe Miss O'Hara is awake. She was mighty restless and I saw her put more wood on the fire a few minutes ago."

"Why are you telling me this, Private?"

"She, ah . . . she spoke to me, sir. Told me to tell you to wake her if she was asleep when you came in. She wants to talk to you, I think."

"Very good, Rivers. On your way, now."

Rivers mounted up and rode off into the night.

Zak waited until he was well gone and then started walking toward the adobe. Before he got to the door, Colleen stepped out. She had a shawl wrapped around her shoulders, a bandanna covering her hair.

"Take a short walk?" she said. "Before you turn in?"

"Sure, Colleen," he said, offering her his arm.

She slipped her arm through his and they walked out on the plain.

"You smell nice," he said.

"I keep lilac water with me. To freshen up."

"Yes, you smell of lilacs."

"It's nice of you to notice."

"Can't sleep, Colleen?"

"Oh, I lay down. Dozed. But . . ."

"But what?"

She stopped, and so did he.

"I — I keep thinking about you," she said. "I hate myself for judging you. For accusing you of things."

"It's all right."

"No it isn't," she said. "You're such a mystery to me. I — I've never met a man like you, Zak. You're — You're . . . oh, I don't know, a kind of enigma, a puzzle I can't quite figure out."

"Is it necessary to figure everybody out?"

"Not everybody, silly, just you. And, yes, I think it's necessary. I was attracted to you the first moment I saw you. I felt . . . something. I don't know what it was, but I was drawn to you. Like a moth to a flame."

"You were at Fort Bowie. Plenty of male companionship available."

She sighed.

He smelled her faint perfume, and it added a pleasing dimension to the night. She looked lovely in the moonlight, even shrouded up as she was. She could be feminine wearing a burlap sack for a dress, he thought, a ragweed crown for a hat.

"Average men," she said, "with average thoughts. And, by average thoughts, I mean —"

"I know what you mean, Colleen."

"See? You do know what I mean. The men

I met at Fort Bowie were mostly obtuse. Do you know the meaning of that word?"

"Yes. You had no feelings for them. They were just faces and forms. Like blocks of wood, pieces of lumber."

"Straw men, more accurately."

They both laughed.

She touched his arm and they gazed at each other. He felt a longing in her that matched his own. Perhaps it was the night and the quiet, but he felt drawn to her. She was a puzzle herself, he thought. She had strong opinions and she had a tongue as sharp as any fishwife's, but she was also gentle and sweet and very alluring.

"Colleen," he said, catching his senses up from his romantic reverie, "this . . . this attraction, or whatever you want to call it, whatever it is, can't go anywhere. You and I come from two different worlds. You're a schoolteacher, refined, educated, genteel, even. I'm a rough man used to rough living. That bark on me is going to stay on me until I die."

"Don't talk like that, Zak. You're much more than that. You — You would fit in anywhere. You could be an important man. With the right woman. I sense that about you."

"You would have me change to suit you,

your idea of me," he said, and knew it was true.

"No, I didn't mean it that way, Zak. I just mean, well, you won't always be doing what you're doing. Chasing bad men. Shooting and killing. There's a better side to you. I know there is."

"I am what I am, Colleen."

"You're stubborn, too," she said.

"Maybe. But I think you may be missing the point. I've chosen this life I lead. I was given life and I cherish it. But one thing I don't want is to fit into somebody else's mold. I would be tempted, with a beautiful woman like you, but I know it would never work. If I was transplanted to a city and a house with a fence around it, little children at my feet, I'd always be looking over the fence, the horizon, and wishing I were back on the Great Plains, hunting buffalo, running with the Lakota, sitting at a Cheyenne campfire, catching trout high in the Rocky Mountains. I'm wild, Colleen, as wild as they come, and I could never settle in one place and assume a respectability I never had, or ever wanted."

"You sound so sure of yourself, Zak. But it seems to me that you are fighting with yourself, deep inside, fighting against who you are, the life you've chosen for yourself."

"No, Colleen. I'm happy with who I am and what I do. You must understand that."

She sighed again.

"I don't think I ever could," she said. "Not after knowing you as I have, even for so brief a time."

"Just live in the moment, Colleen. Don't try and look into the future. All the life we have is just this one single moment. And this moment is forever. That's something I learned from the Lakota. Life is a journey and it's a circle. We follow our paths and when we come to the end it's another beginning."

"I don't know if I understand you," she said.

"No matter. Someday you'll remember what I said tonight and it might even make sense."

"I don't want to quarrel with you anymore."

"Then we won't. This journey we're on now is strange for you. It's as if we're in a different world, both of us, and the rules of civilization and decency have been left by the wayside. We'll finish the journey, and we will have learned something, you and I. But after that, we must say good-bye to each other. You will go your way, and I will go mine."

"You make it sound so final."

"We have the moment," he said. "This moment."

He took her in his arms and kissed her. It was a long, lingering kiss, and she pressed against him until he could feel her warmth, the pulse of her being. He felt dizzy with rapture, and the scent of lilacs wafted to his nostrils and made him feel giddy and aroused.

"Oh," she said, when they broke the kiss. "Oh, my. That — That was wonderful."

"Can you sleep now, Colleen?"

"I — I don't know. Maybe. I wish there was more, though."

"Just this moment, Colleen. No other."

They walked back together, arm in arm. He felt an odd sense of contentment, but he knew that nothing had been resolved. Perhaps nothing ever would be.

But they had had that moment, and for now it was enough for him.

He slept, waking only when the watch changed, and then fell back asleep, dreaming of lilac fields and wild horses, the shining mountains, silver streams that sang as they coursed through steep rocky canyons, and soft snow on the high peaks, a woman dressed in a bearskin and children rolling hoops and chasing after them with sticks that turned into wriggling snakes.

Just before dawn he heard a commotion, and a man groaned in pain. He sat up and reached for his pistol.

"Get the bastard," Rivers shouted, and Zak saw a dark shape looming over him. One of the prisoners had freed himself and disarmed Rivers.

Colleen screamed in terror.

O'Hara struggled to his feet and was knocked down.

The man, carrying a rifle, hurtled straight toward Zak. The rifle was pointed at him.

He heard the lever work and a shell slide into the firing chamber, the hammer lock in place on full cock.

The horses outside whinnied, and his hand flew to the butt of his pistol.

He wondered if he would have time. He wondered, in that split second of eternity, if he would ever have time to keep his own death at bay.

His arm felt numb from sleeping on it and his fingers were rubbery and nearly lifeless.

Time. Was there enough time to draw and shoot?

All he could do was try.

That was all any man could do.

Time be damned.

CHAPTER 26

Zak raised his pistol just far enough to fire at Pablo Medina. He hoped the man would run into his bullet. A moment after pulling the trigger, he ducked and rolled to one side. He heard the explosion from the rifle, so close the sound was deafening. The bullet ripped into his bedroll and plowed a furrow in the dirt floor.

Medina grunted as Zak's pistol bullet smashed into his lower abdomen. He pitched forward, the rifle falling from his hands, as the bullet crushed veins and capillaries, mashed flesh into pulp and nicked his spine before blowing a fist-sized hole in his back.

He cried out in pain, and hit the floor screaming at the top of his lungs.

He kept screaming as Zak raised up, cocked his pistol again and took aim at Medina's head, ready to fire from a distance of three feet.

"Kill him," Rivers shouted.

Scofield drew his pistol, crouched a few feet away from the fallen man.

Colleen put her hands to her ears, shrank against the wall as if trying to escape the hideous screams, the gushing blood that pooled on both sides of Medina.

Zak held his fire, his gaze fixed on Medina, who kept screaming, his back arched as if he were gripped in the vise of a seizure.

Hoofbeats pounded on the ground outside, and a moment later Ted O'Hara burst through the door, slamming it back against the wall. He crouched low, a rifle in his hands, his head moving from side to side.

"What in hell's going on in here?" he said.

"Get out of the doorway, Ted," Zak said. "Medina tried to escape."

O'Hara saw the man on the floor, then looked toward his sister, who was still pinned against the wall, a small fist in her mouth.

He sidled to one side, still in a crouch. He seemed like a coiled spring, ready to pounce.

Medina continued to scream.

"Do something, Zak," Colleen said, taking her fist from her mouth.

"Yeah," Scofield said, "put that poor

bastard out of his misery, will you, Colonel?"

Zak considered that suggestion. It would seem the humane thing to do. Under the circumstances. Blood poured out of Medina's back wound, little spurts ejecting with every beat of his heart. The screaming wasn't helping any, either. Pump, bleed, pump, he thought.

He leaned over and clamped a hand over Medina's mouth, shutting off his scream.

"Callate," he said.

Medina swallowed his scream, but sweat broke out on his forehead, and the muscles in his face expanded and contracted with the pain he felt all through his body. Zak drew his hand away.

"Ayudame, por favor. Me duele mucho." Help me, please. I am hurting very much. There was an agonized pleading in Medina's voice.

Zak snapped his fingers, looked back at Rivers.

"Bring me a small piece of kindling wood," he said. "Quick."

Rivers, paralyzed until that moment, jumped toward the stove, reached down and picked up a small sliver of wood. He took it to Zak, handed it to him.

Zak stuck the wood inside Medina's mouth.

"Bite on it," he said, in Spanish.

Medina bit down and tears streamed from his eyes.

"Thank God," breathed Colleen.

O'Hara walked over to Zak, stood over Medina, then looked at Rivers.

"How did this man get loose, Private?" he asked.

"Sir, I don't know. He — He untied the ropes around his ankles and managed to free his hands. He did it real quiet. I didn't know he was loose. He jumped me, grabbed the rifle out of my hands."

"You weren't watching him close enough, Rivers."

"No, sir."

Rivers retreated to the back of the adobe shack.

Zak got to his feet.

"Can we do anything for him, Zak?" O'Hara asked.

"He's losing blood fast. My bullet must have cut an artery. Not all of the blood is coming out his back."

"He's bleeding to death, then."

"It looks that way."

O'Hara turned his head. He could not look at the dying man. Colleen remained cowering against the wall, her gaze fixed on Zak. Scofield's face was a mask of hatred and contempt as he gazed down at Medina.

Zak eased the hammer down on his pistol but didn't put it back in its holster.

"I think this man's paralyzed," he said. "Bullet probably sheared off part of his backbone."

"He's not moving much, with all that pain," O'Hara said.

Morning light began to seep in through the windows. Medina groaned, but he didn't spit out the stick and scream. Zak felt pity for the man. At the same time, he thought of how often men made mistakes in judgment that cost them their lives, or crippled them for life. Medina was probably bleeding to death, but his last minutes on earth would be agonizing. The man should have known better. What caused someone like him to think he could get away like that? Loyalty to Ferguson, or to Trask? Or was he like some cornered animal, so hungry for freedom that he would risk his life to escape? Well, Medina had lost. The risk had been too great.

Zak saw the light spreading across the landscape, turning the rocks to rust, casting shadows to the west, pulling all the cool from the earth. In the distance he heard the call of a quail, and he saw a pair of doves fly across the barren land, twisting in the air like dancers with wings.

"Scofield, you and Rivers start carrying wood outside. Everything that will burn — tables, chairs, firewood. Pile them up nearby at the highest point of the land. Break the furniture up if you have to. Build me a tall pyramid." Zak turned to Colleen. "If you have any female things to do, Colleen, best get to it. We're leaving."

"What about Pablo there?" she asked.

"What about him?"

"Are you just going to leave him lying there in agony?"

"There's nothing I can do for him," Zak said.

"So, you're just going to watch him die. In agony."

"I'm not going to watch him die."

"But he's going to die," she said.

"Yes."

"Oh, you . . ." She flounced out of the adobe, into the dawn. He heard her rummaging through her saddlebags at the hitchrail. There was a rustle of paper, the ruffle and flap of cloth, footsteps on the hard cool ground.

Medina retched and spat the stick onto the dirt floor. Blood bubbled up out of the hole in his back.

"We better move him," O'Hara said.

"Grab an arm," Zak said.

The two men pulled Medina away from the vomit. Zak turned him over so he lay on his back. His face was wet with tears, his eyes glistening like ebony agates.

"I do not feel my legs," Medina said, in English.

"Do you feel pain?" Zak asked.

"No more." This, in Spanish.

"You're paralyzed, Pablo," Zak said. "If you know any prayers, say them."

"There is no priest."

"No. There's just you and God."

Medina began to weep, without shame. Zak and O'Hara looked at each other. O'Hara shook his head. Zak nodded.

"You just goin' to leave me back here?" Deets said from the rear of the room.

"Take him outside, Ted," Zak said. "I'll be out soon. Have Rivers and Scofield knock down those hitchrails and stack them with the other wood. There should be a maul or a hammer in here somewhere, a pry bar, maybe."

"Will do," O'Hara said. He walked to the back of the adobe and looked around for something to tear down the hitchrails. He found an old sledgehammer, picked it up.

Then he walked over to Deets, untied the rope around his ankles and stood him up.

"You run, Deets," O'Hara said, "I'll shoot you down."

Deets growled low in his throat but said no words.

The two men walked outside.

Zak heard voices as O'Hara gave commands and Scofield answered him. Rivers came in and carried out a table. He came back for a chair.

"You want us to tear apart these bunk beds?" he asked Zak.

"Everything that will burn, Hugh."

"First time you've called me by my first name," Rivers said. "It's Hugo, not Hugh."

"All right, Hugo. What's in a name, anyway?"

"Huh?"

"Never mind," Zak said.

Rivers was outside for some moments. Zak heard Scofield lay into the hitchrails with the sledge. Apparently Rivers spelled him, because Scofield entered the adobe to carry out another chair, a shelf board, and a wooden box.

"Pile's gettin' pretty big," he said to Zak, who still stood over Medina.

"Keep stacking it up, Scofield."

"Yes, sir."

Medina stopped crying. He put a hand to his face and rubbed his cheeks.

"There is pain now," he said, his voice a whispery rasp. This was in Spanish, and Zak spoke to him in Spanish.

"Did you pray, Pablo?"

"Yes. I will die soon, maybe."

"Maybe."

"You do not shoot me? To make it quick?"

"No. You're going to have to die on your own, Pablo."

"I want to die now. Give me a gun."

"You are Catholic, Pablo?"

"Yes."

"Is it not a mortal sin for a man to take his own life?"

"I think so, yes. But the pain . . . it is so much now."

"If there is no priest, to whom do you confess, Pablo?"

"Maybe to God. Maybe to you."

"Better God than me."

"Maybe," he said. "I will confess."

"Ask to be forgiven for your sins," Zak said.

"Yes, I will do that."

"The dying will be your penance."

"What?" The man's eyes glittered behind the tears.

"Does not the priest give you penance?

Prayers to say, good deeds to do?"

"Yes, the priest does that. He says to say the Hail Marys, the Our Fathers. So many for so many sins."

"Say those, then. It will take your mind off the pain, perhaps."

Medina closed his eyes. Zak could see his lips quivering, opening slightly and closing again, as if he was murmuring the prayers or confessing. Then he heard the word *peccata* and realized that Pablo was speaking in Latin, that ancient, dead language that was never spoken until the Catholic priests took up the practice.

A Jesuit had told Zak about Latin, how it was always only a written language until the priests spoke the Mass in that tongue. The priest had studied Latin and spoken it for two years before he took his vows. The language was precise, highly inflected, and suited the Church's purposes. Zak believed that the Church made the language sacred and holy to separate themselves from ordinary people, add mystery to their canons. And now Pablo Medina was talking to his God in the Latin. Somehow, it seemed fitting. Zak saw blood streaming from underneath him and the color seemed to drain from his face. His lips paled and stopped moving.

"Good-bye, Pablo," Zak said, in Spanish. "Go with God."

Medina crossed himself with pathetically slow movements and then all the strength seemed to leave him. His arm flopped down and lay across his chest.

But then, when Zak thought he was gone, Medina gasped and a shiver coursed through his torso. He opened his eyes wide and looked up as if seeing a phantasm. He choked, gasped, then let out a last breath. His mouth opened, but he did not breathe anymore.

"Vaya con Dios," Zak said again, and turned away.

He walked outside and drew a deep breath. The air was clean and cool. The desert scents wafted to his nostrils and filled him with an odd warmth.

Colleen walked up from where she had been, beyond the road. She was carrying a small towel, a canteen, a bottle of lilac water, and a bundle of sanitaries.

"Can you make us some coffee before we go, Colleen?" Zak asked.

"Yes. The stove is hot, we've water and a pot. Do you have a cup?"

"In my saddlebags."

O'Hara and Deets were up above them on the slight ridge, watching the soldiers break the legs off tables and chairs, pile them atop a pyramid of wood.

"Is Pablo . . ." Colleen's eyes bore into Zak's, searched his face.

"He's gone, Colleen."

"Thank God," she said.

"God had nothing to do with it," he said, a trace of bitterness in his tone.

She started to retort, but saw the look on Zak's face and swept past him, disappeared inside the adobe. Another pair of doves whistled past, and the thin high clouds glistened white and peach in the morning sun. Zak looked to the east, to the land of the Chiricahua, and thought of Cochise.

Now there, he thought, was a man to ride the river with.

And they both had one more river to cross.

CHAPTER 27

Zak carried a flaming faggot out to the pile of wood.

"After this gets going," he said to Rivers and Scofield, "cut down all the cactus, cholla, yucca, and whatever else is green and throw it on the blaze and then we'll get the hell out of here."

He threw the chunk of blazing kindling into the pile of wood, near the bottom of the pyramid, and watched as the flames licked at the fuel. O'Hara, Colleen, and Deets stood by, drinking their coffees, watching the wood catch fire.

"Mind telling me what this is all about, Zak?" O'Hara asked.

"I hope it'll be a signal fire, Ted."

"A signal fire? For whom, if I may ask?"

"For Cochise."

"Cochise? Did I hear you right?"

Ted almost choked on his coffee. Colleen, too, looked surprised. Deets stood there with a dumb look on his face. He'd stopped bleeding and Zak had untied the rope around his wrists. He, too, was drinking coffee. Another of Zak's acts of kindness toward his prisoner.

"You heard me, Ted. We're going to need Cochise."

"What will he make of the fire?"

"I expect one of his scouts will see the smoke when it starts rising. Cochise will want to know what it's about."

"That seems like a pretty long shot to me," O'Hara said.

The first plumes of smoke began to lift off the pyre. They were thin at that point, but as Scofield and Rivers threw green plants on the top, the smoke spread out and thickened. Soon, the fire was blazing and smoke spiraled up to the sky, spreading as the zephyrs caught it.

"Now, go inside the adobe and bring those bunk mattresses out," Zak told the soldiers. "Toss them on the fire and then mount up."

"Yes, sir," Rivers and Scofield chorused.

Zak finished his coffee while the soldiers piled on the damp mattresses. The feathers crackled and fumed, adding bulk to the rising smoke. A tower of black and gray smoke above the blaze, smoke that could be seen for miles around.

He put his cup back in his saddlebags. "Mount up," he ordered.

Colleen and Ted tossed the rest of their coffee onto the ground. In moments they were mounted, along with Rivers, Scofield, and Deets.

"Deets, you can light a shuck," Zak told his prisoner.

"Huh?"

"Go on. Ride up that road and tell Trask anything you want."

"You mean you're just turnin' me loose? I can go?"

"Nobody's going to shoot you in the back, Deets. Go on. I have no further interest in you."

For a moment Deets appeared unsure of himself. He looked at O'Hara, who gave no indication of approval or disapproval. He looked at Rivers and Scofield. Their faces were impassive.

Then he clucked to his horse and turned him toward the road.

He stopped, turned back to look at Zak.

"You really going to sic Cochise on us, Mr. Cody?"

"You bet your boots I am, Deets."

Zak smiled, but there was no warmth in it. It was the kind of smile that would curdle milk, or the blood in a man's veins. Deets turned and rode off slowly toward the road. Everyone around the fire watched him go.

"That was a big mistake, Zak," O'Hara said. "You'll lose the element of surprise."

"I want Trask to know his days are numbered," Zak said.

"You might be numbering our days," O'Hara said.

Zak ticked spurs into Nox's flanks. He rode off to the east, the others following. He could still smell the smoke, and he knew the fire would burn long enough to serve its purpose.

He took an angle, away from the road, straight into the heart of Chiricahua country. He had cleaned his pistol, oiled it, reloaded it with six brass cartridges. His rifle, too, was loaded and ready. He knew that because of his wound, Deets could not travel fast. By the time Deets reached that last old stage station, Zak figured he would be smoking the pipe with Cochise. And, maybe, Jeffords would be there, too. The more the merrier.

Quail piped and he saw a coyote slink toward the shack they had just left, its nose to the ground, its tail drooping. The coyote was a gray shadow on the landscape, a ghost left over from the dark night and the flash flood. A survivor, slat-ribbed, lean, scavenging for scraps, leftovers, and maybe a dead man lying inside the adobe, his scent already rising, like the smoke from the fire, to alert the buzzards that were already circling in the sky.

Cochise would see them, too.

Everything was perfect, Zak thought. Just as he had planned.

Chapter 28

Lieutenant John Welch needed only one glance at the map Ben Trask had spread out on the table.

"That's Lieutenant O'Hara's map, all right," he said. "That's his writing on it."

Trask smiled with satisfaction. He jabbed a finger down on one of the X's O'Hara had drawn.

"And that's where we'll find Cochise and his whole damned tribe. Think you can find it, Lieutenant?"

"You're damned right I can find it. He's got compass directions, everything we need. I'm ready to go if you are. Looks to be about a two-day ride. Three at most."

"Let's do it," Trask said.

They walked out of the adobe together. Welch's troops were mounted, and Ferguson stood by on horseback with his men and Trask's. He held the reins of Trask's horse. Trask took them and climbed into the saddle.

Ferguson was looking off toward the west, his eyes squinted to narrow slits.

Trask adjusted his boots in the stirrups, looked off in the same direction that Ferguson was gazing.

"What are you looking at?" he asked.

"Smoke," Ferguson said. "Way off."

"I wonder what it means," Trask said.

"I have no idea," Ferguson replied.

Welch barked the orders and his troops moved out in a column of twos. There was no guidon, and all of the troops, including Welch, wore civilian clothes. The only clues that the men were in the army were their rifles and their boots. Otherwise, they looked like any group of ordinary townfolk.

"Did you see all that smoke in the sky over to the west of us, Trask?" Welch said after a few minutes.

"Yeah, I saw it."

"What do you make of it?"

"Something caught fire."

"Looks to be somewhere near the old stage road."

"Could be."

"It doesn't worry you?"

"Why should it? It's miles away. Hell, I've seen smoke all my life. There's always somebody burnin' something, leaves, trash, you name it."

"Not likely anybody's burning leaves in this country," Welch said.

"I've seen 'em burn dead horses and dead cattle, too," Trask said.

"Up north, you see smoke like that, you think one thing. I'm talking about Colorado, Montana, the Dakotas."

"Yeah. Injuns."

"That's right," Welch said.

"So, did you ever see Apaches send smoke signals?" Trask asked.

"No, but I've only been here about a year."

"Don't worry about it, then. I ain't."

Welch looked at him.

Trask had the bark on him, all right. But the smoke gave Welch an uneasy feeling. He looked around at the wide sky, the blueness of it so pretty it could make a man's eyes well up, and the little puffs of clouds. As pretty a day as he'd ever seen.

But there shouldn't have been smoke to smudge that pretty blue sky.

CHAPTER 29

They rode past the sunset and through the long night, Zak in the lead. Scofield slept in the saddle, with Rivers making sure he didn't fall from his horse. Ted let his sister sleep as she rode, and he kept close, ready to catch her if she fell. Rivers and Scofield took turns, but neither truly slept. They just kept going.

Zak stopped every four hours so everyone could walk around and stretch. Toward morning he halted to build a fire, make coffee. The coffee kept them going, and when dawn broke they were on horseback once again, riding straight into the rising, blinding sun.

Near noon Zak took out his silver dollar and began flashing it like a signal mirror. An hour later he got an answer. Three flashes. He tipped the dollar and sent back three flashes. A single flash answered him, which he also acknowledged.

They all saw the flashes.

"You know who that is, Zak?" O'Hara asked.

"I think so. Wait."

Zak flashed the coin again. There were answering flashes.

He put the silver dollar back in his pocket.

"Well?" O'Hara said.

"That was Anillo. 'Ring,' in English. He told me a place to meet. Cochise will be there."

"How far? How long?" The news seemed to give O'Hara new energy. He was as bright-eyed as a recruit after his first shave.

"One hour. At an Apache well I know. They know I'm coming with you, your sister, and two bluecoat soldiers."

O'Hara laughed. "I'm glad I made friends with Cochise."

"Yes. He will listen to us. Now, do you know where Trask and Welch might be going?"

"I know exactly where they're going, if they follow the map I marked for Trask. I think Cochise will know it, too. Maybe you, too, know it."

"Tell me about it, Ted."

"I picked this place because of a story an old Apache told me when we passed by it. It is an open area with a narrow entrance.

The plain is surrounded by low hills. The chief at the time, a man named Lobo, lured the soldiers there. He made it look like a camp. The soldiers meant to wipe out the Apaches. The Apaches hid behind the little hills, and after the soldiers entered the box canyon, the Chiricahua sealed it off with many braves. When the soldiers started shooting at the lodges, the Apaches rose up all around and fired arrows down at the soldiers. The soldiers who tried to ride back out were met by men with lances and bows and were cut down. I didn't know whether to believe the old man, but I can't forget that place. When Trask asked me where he could find Cochise and his gold, that's the spot I marked on the map."

"That was smart of you, Ted."

"Do you know the place?"

"I do. The Apaches call it the Canyon of Blood."

"Yes, that's it."

"Perfect," Zak said.

An hour later there arose a hush over the land. O'Hara felt it and glanced around, an apprehensive look on his face.

Rivers and Scofield went quiet, too, and began scanning the land all around them.

"It's so quiet," Colleen said. "All of a sudden."

Then she let out a cry as a nearly naked man emerged out of the dust and rock ahead of her, his face painted for war, a rifle in his hands, a pistol hanging from his waist.

"That would be Anillo," Zak said. He raised his right hand in greeting.

"He — He nearly scared me to death," Colleen said in a breathy whisper.

Anillo held up his hand, then turned and ran at a lope up a slight rise.

Zak looked at the sky.

It was not yet noon. The place where Trask was headed, Blood Canyon, was no more than a few hours from where they now were. Time to get there, maybe, before Trask arrived, and set the trap for him, a trap that O'Hara had practically guaranteed.

Time enough for Trask to experience what Zak called an Apache sunset.

As they topped the hill, O'Hara, Colleen, Scofield, and Rivers all gasped at the sight.

There were the Chiricahuas, all mounted on their ponies, their faces daubed in bright colors, the colors of war.

And greeting Zak with open arms was a most impressive man, the fiercest one of them all.

Cochise.

CHAPTER 30

They sat in a circle, on blankets laid down by the Chiricahua. Cochise puffed on the pipe, blew the smoke to the four directions, passed it to Tesoro, who passed it to his son, Anillo. The pipe was passed to O'Hara, then to Scofield, Rivers, and finally to Cody.

Zak presented Pablo Medina's rifle and pistol to Cochise, who took them, hefted them, and grinned in appreciation. Next, Zak gave a rifle and pistol to Anillo, items that had once belonged to Al Deets. He handed them pistol and rifle cartridges. The conversation was in Spanish.

"It is good to see Red Hair again," Cochise said to O'Hara.

"It is my honor to be with the great Cochise," Ted said.

"And, my brother, Shadow Rider, it is good that you are here."

"We come, Cochise, to ask you to help us stop a war with the white men. We wish to go to the Canyon of Blood."

"We will fight there?" Cochise said.

"Yes."

"Who do we fight?"

"We will take the rifles and pistols from many white men. Red Hair will arrest these men and return them to Fort Bowie, where they will stand trial."

"You do not want us to kill these white men?"

"I will give you one white man. You will take this man to an Apache sundown."

"Ah, that is good, Shadow Rider."

"Let us do this now, Cochise. We must be at the Canyon of Blood before the white men come. We must give them a surprise. I do not want blood to be spilled."

"You talk of war without blood, Shadow Rider."

"That is what I want. If we do this, the Chiricahua can live in peace on their own lands."

When the ceremonies were over, Zak rode with O'Hara and Cochise, while the warriors rode single file ahead of them. In the rear, Colleen was flanked by Rivers and Scofield.

They reached the small entrance to the canyon by mid-afternoon.

"This is the place," O'Hara said. "It appears to be deserted."

"Look off to the south," Zak said. "Toward Fort Bowie."

O'Hara shaded his eyes and stared at the land for several seconds.

"I don't see anything," he said. "Just empty land. Not even a bird."

"Just above the land, Ted. It's faint, but it's there."

Cochise was looking in the same direction.

O'Hara stiffened. "I see it," he said. "Is that dust?"

"That's dust. Men are riding this way, and they're in a hurry."

The dust was a faint scrim just above the horizon. The way the sun caught it, the particles shimmered a reddish color, turning a tawny yellow, then back to rose.

"The dust is far," Cochise said.

"Do you remember the battle here, Cochise?" Zak asked the Chiricahua chief. "Do you remember the story?"

"I remember. We will do as my fathers did."

Cochise deployed his braves behind the small hills. Anillo and a small band flanked the entrance to the shallow canyon, covering themselves with dirt and lying flat among the desert plants.

"Put Colleen behind that little hill at the farthest end, Ted," Zak said, "and tell her to stay put. You and I, Scofield and Rivers, will be the gate that closes on Trask and his bunch once they enter the canyon."

"I don't see —"

Zak pointed to a series of small mounds about fifty yards from the entrance. "We'll leave our horses with Colleen and walk there, become like the Apaches.

"You mean lie down in the dirt."

"That's what I mean," Zak said.

In less than fifteen minutes there wasn't an Apache to be seen. Zak and O'Hara, along with Rivers and Scofield, lay behind the mounds, hats off, concealed by bushes and cactus.

The dust cloud in the sky grew larger.

Zak put his ear to the ground. He could hear the pounding hoofbeats. He knew that the Chiricahua were all doing the same. The Apaches would be able to gauge the distance, and they would be ready.

So would he.

In the stillness, a quail piped a warning as the riders approached. Zak saw them and his heart began to pound in his chest. He looked at Ted and put a finger to his lips. Ted nodded.

Trask, Ferguson, and Welch were at the

head of the column. Trask had a map in his hands, while Welch studied a compass.

"That's the place," Trask said, his voice loud enough to carry to where Zak waited. Cochise knew what to do. If it worked, it would all be over in a matter of minutes. And no blood would be spilled.

Everything, though, had to work just right.

Zak watched as Trask galloped into the canyon. The riders behind him all filed in, disappeared from Zak's view.

"Now," he said, and got to his feet. O'Hara, Rivers, and Scofield all leaped to their feet and followed Zak as he ran toward the entrance. Anillo and six braves appeared like magic out of nowhere, and close by, Tesoro and his men sprouted out of the ground.

At the same time, as Zak and his group joined up with Tesoro and Anillo, Apaches with rifles appeared on the tops of the small hills, their rifles aimed at the outlaws and soldiers. Trask reined in, and all of the men halted their horses. For a long moment they all seemed to be frozen. They looked like statues or figures in a painting.

Zak strode into the silent arena.

"Throw down your weapons," he said. "You are surrounded. If you don't, the

Apaches will kill every one of you, to a man."

His voice seemed to echo as it traveled from one end of the canyon to the other.

"Do it now, Trask," Zak shouted, "or I'll order Cochise and his men to blow you all out of your saddles."

Trask turned to Welch and Ferguson. Zak couldn't hear him, but knew he was talking it over.

"Now," Zak shouted.

The Apaches on the hills leaned toward the men below, rifles at their shoulders. Trask looked at both ends of the canyon and saw the Apaches, O'Hara, Scofield and Rivers.

"Hands up," Zak ordered, and a dozen Spencers fell to the ground. Hands flew up into the air. More rifles clattered to the ground. The last to surrender was Trask, but the Apaches had him cold, and he knew it.

Zak motioned to Anillo and Tesoro to follow him. O'Hara, Rivers, and Scofield trotted to catch up to him.

Apaches streamed down from the hillocks into the bloodless arena.

"You bastard," Trask said when Zak walked up to him.

"Get off your horse, Trask."

In seconds all of the men were surrounded by Apaches. O'Hara and the two soldiers under his command began to take their pistols.

Trask dismounted. "What are you going to do with us?" he asked Zak.

"Some of the Apaches are going to escort Lieutenant O'Hara and his prisoners back to Fort Bowie. You're staying here, with Cochise. You came after the gold, didn't you?"

Trask was speechless.

Some Apaches brought horses, and many began to mount their ponies. Others gathered up the rifles and pistols, exclaiming their pleasure at the trophies that had fallen into their hands.

Colleen rode in, leading their horses. Her eyes were wide with wonder. She sat there, looking down at Zak.

Zak grabbed Trask by the collar and took him over to Cochise.

"You're going to experience an Apache sundown, Trask," he said. "Think of it as my hole card. What you draw next is going to bust your flush."

"Huh?" Trask said. "What's an Apache sundown?"

"You don't know what an Apache sundown is, Trask? That's when a Chiricahua stakes you out on an anthill early in the morning, pours sugar water all over your buck naked body, daubs it in your nose and eyes and ears, in your mouth. Ants go crazy over anything sweet. They'll swarm all over you and start eating you from the inside out. You'll scream until sundown, if you last that long, and beg for an Apache war club to dash your brains to strawberry jam. After sundown you can't scream any more and your light goes out, permanent. It's sundown for you on this life, and old Sol is never going to rise on you again, because by morning the critters will eat you down to bones, and what the coyotes and buzzards miss, the worms will take care of, over time. It's better than you deserve, Trask, and maybe Hell won't be so bad at first."

"You bastard," Trask said as the Apaches led him away.

O'Hara let out a breath.

"Well, Zak," he said, "you pulled it off. I didn't think it was possible, but . . ."

"We'll see to it that these men and Willoughby get a court-martial."

"I didn't see Deets among these men," O'Hara said.

Zak laughed.

"We'll probably find him waiting at that last line shack. He might as well be punished with the rest of them."

Colleen frowned.

"Will you be around to testify?" she said.

"No, I won't be there, Colleen. As soon as I deliver these men to Fort Bowie, I'll be riding on. The judge can read my report in court."

"Just like that? You're riding on?"

"Yes. I'll say good-bye, first, of course."

"It's always good-bye with you, isn't it, Zak?"

Her eyes were misting and there was a catch in her throat. He hated to break her heart, but he could never live in her world.

He didn't answer. He didn't have to.

Yes, with him, he thought, it was always good-bye.

But this one would be the hardest good-bye of them all.

ABOUT THE AUTHOR

Jory Sherman won the Spur Award for *The Medicine Horn,* and authored the Barons Saga. He died in 2014.

The employees of Thorndike Press hope you have enjoyed this Large Print book. All our Thorndike, Wheeler, and Kennebec Large Print titles are designed for easy reading, and all our books are made to last. Other Thorndike Press Large Print books are available at your library, through selected bookstores, or directly from us.

For information about titles, please call:
(800) 223-1244

or visit our website at:
gale.com/thorndike

To share your comments, please write:
Publisher
Thorndike Press
10 Water St., Suite 310
Waterville, ME 04901